Dept. of
Reproductive Management

Kelly A. Wilson

Brown Dog Publishing

Dept. of Reproductive Management
Copyright © 2014 by Kelly A. Wilson

ISBN-13 978-0692282045
ISBN- 10 0692282041

Cover design and art by Slobodan Cedic
Copyright © 2014

For more information:
www.kellywilsonbooks.com

to
the **Queen** & the **Admiral**

You gave me the courage to follow my dreams.
And despite the odds, you can still picture the greenhouse.

Dept. of
Reproductive Management

Kelly A. Wilson

Brown Dog Publishing

Chapter One

September 2056

Henry paced hurriedly as panic set in. "We need to get you to the hospital."

"No…we agreed," Liz said between quick breaths. Her contractions had started several hours ago, but they were getting worse. The sheets on the bed, as well as her clothes, were completely soaked through with sweat.

"The contractions are coming too fast."

"No, it's—" She let out a piercing scream. Henry stared, horrorstruck, but she didn't need to ask why. She saw the blood right as dizziness hit, and then she was gone.

Liz awoke in a bright room. People were all around her but she didn't recognize any of them. A woman stopped, noticing she was awake. "Don't worry, dear, you're at the hospital."

"The hospital?" Liz panicked. "What happened?"

"Your baby was in distress. If your husband hadn't gotten you here when he did, things could've turned out differently."

"My husband?" She took several deep breaths as she tried to focus. "The baby?"

"We had to do an emergency C-section, but the baby is fine. A very healthy little girl. 7 pounds, 6 ounces."

Liz smiled. "Can I see her?"

The nurse nodded and stepped away, returning moments later with a small baby in her arms. Gently, Liz took the child. Never before had she so instantly been in love with something. "She's adorable."

"Looks just like her mother." The nurse smiled. "Now, I suppose it might be better to ask your husband, but I will need all of your paperwork."

Her heart skipped a beat. That was the reason they wanted to avoid the hospital. "Paperwork, yes."

"I realize you arrived in quite a rush. We can look it up by name if that would be preferable."

"Can I see my husband?" Liz asked.

The nurse frowned. "Ma'am, I can let you see him, but I must inform you that if you refuse to give me this information, I will be forced to call the DRM."

"No, don't call them." She shook her head. "We have everything."

As the nurse left, Liz's mind whirled. Their only chance was to get out of the hospital as soon as possible.

"Thank God you're all right," Henry said as he

entered the room.

"Why did you bring me here?" she asked as soon as the nurse left. "We have to get out of here. See if there are any clothes in the closet."

"I'm sorry, I had no other choice." He searched the wardrobe in the corner of the room but he could only find hospital scrubs. "These will have to do."

She got out of bed, still feeling very weak. With each movement, the fresh skin used to seal the deep cuts from surgery pulled excruciatingly, and she worried she would rip the synthetic fabric.

"She's adorable." Liz looked up to see Henry staring at their little girl.

"I think I have the perfect name for her too."

"What's that?"

"Charlotte."

He smiled. "I love it."

Without warning, the door opened and four men in dark uniforms entered.

"Good Evening. I am Lieutenant Nathan Wilcox with the Department of Reproductive Management. May I please see your papers? It is standard routine with any pregnancy that comes into the emergency room." He was young, in his late twenties, but clearly experienced. He'd done this before.

Henry and Liz looked at each other, neither sure what to say.

"We don't have it," he answered finally. "We left in

such a rush that I forgot it at home."

"That's understandable. Luckily, we can now look everything up by name." Lieutenant Wilcox pulled a small tablet from the side pocket of his pants. "According to your admission records, you have yet to give your personal information."

"Well, you see—" Liz began.

"Let me be frank, ma'am. If you do not provide the necessary paperwork or allow us to access it, I'll have no choice but to take you both into custody."

She looked to Henry who was standing so close to baby Charlotte. Just beyond where their daughter slept was a second door, the only other way out of the room. There was nothing between him and escape. She took a deep breath, knowing how badly she was about to hurt herself, and then threw her body into the Lieutenant, knocking him to the ground.

"Henry, take her and run!"

Without hesitation, he grabbed Charlotte and ran for the door, but the other officers were too quick. One sprinted around the bed and got to the door just as Henry turned toward it. The other officer came up behind him. He was trapped between the two. Lieutenant Wilcox pushed Liz's face down on the floor and pulled her hands behind her back. She screamed in pain as the synthetic skin moved and pulled. Once her hands were secure, Wilcox lifted her to her feet and pushed her to the fourth officer in the room. He gripped her arms painfully tight.

"Henry, was it?" Wilcox asked calmly. Henry's eyes shot between the men surrounding him. "Why don't you put the baby down so we can talk about this like adults."

"I won't let you take her," he said.

"You don't want her to get hurt now, do you?" Wilcox stepped closer.

Liz could see Henry was panicking and the officers were slowly moving forward. She feared they might tackle him and harm Charlotte. "Don't hurt them," she screamed. "I'll tell you who I am, but please don't hurt them."

Wilcox turned to her. "All right, who are you?"

She took a deep breath.

"My name is Elizabeth Fullbrook."

Chapter Two

16 Years Later

Maggie Ward awoke in the same way she did every morning when the siren rang to signal the beginning of the day. Lying in bed, she stared at the white ceiling and listened as the Jessup Reeducation Center came to life once again. Every morning, the sounds were the same. The steady, quiet movements of children being awoken en masse. She took a deep breath and smiled. It was her brother's birthday, and though the center would do nothing to mark the occasion, she had managed to get a special present for him.

She jumped out of bed and dressed, switching from the center's matching white pajamas to the matching blue day clothes. As her roommates slowly filed out of the room, she pulled the hidden treasure from her undersized wardrobe. The chocolate bar was small, only the size of her palm, but it was a luxury. Maggie put it to her nose.

She smiled. "This smells so good."

"And yet, it's delaying my breakfast." Her best friend, Jules, looked at her with both eyebrows raised. Her light brown skin and hazel eyes seemed to pop in contrast to the worn colors of her clothes, and adding her height made her look older than Maggie, despite them being the same age.

"There's always a line if you get there first anyway." Maggie slipped the chocolate bar into her pocket and they left the empty room.

Every hallway and room within Jessup was identical, fluctuating only in size. Dark gray carpet or tiles, gray cement walls, and white ceilings. The Reproductive Management Officers (Remos) said this was to reduce the cost of upkeep stemming from taxpayers' money. For someone new to the Center, it might be frightening or depressing, but Maggie had spent her entire life at Jessup. Along with all the kids there, she had been born illegally.

They walked into the cafeteria with the last of the stragglers, but they were happy to find the line almost gone. As they moved through it, Maggie glanced around the room looking for her brother, but he was nowhere to be found. His roommate, Luke, sat solemnly on his own. Unlike most of the boys at Jessup, Luke had hair so long that it hung in his eyes. It grew at such a fast rate, the Remos had given up trying to keep it cropped short.

"What's wrong with you?" Jules asked as they sat down.

"Mr. Jacobs sent for Ryker early this morning. They didn't say why, but something felt off."

Jules rolled her eyes. "Oh God, not more of this again."

"You tell me when getting sent for by the head of the center is ever a good thing," Luke snapped. They rarely saw Mr. Jacobs. Typically, it was only once a year when he organized a trip for all the children to go to town for dinner and a movie. It was one of the few times they were allowed to leave the center.

"What do you mean, *off*?" Maggie asked.

"It was just strange. They told him to get dressed, to bring his coat, and it took two Remos to get him. It looked like they were worried he might make a run for it."

"Can we please have one day where we don't have a conspiracy theory? Jacobs probably needed some help fixing a fence or something, and Ryker just happens to be strong enough to do it." Jules looked from Luke to Maggie. "Seriously, don't let this guy get you all worked up. He thinks this entire place is out to get him."

"I'm not the only one that thinks that. You'd know the truth about this place if you had any memory of life outside of here," Luke said.

"I'm not getting into this argument again!" Jules' hands flew through the air.

"Guys, stop. We'll just ask Ryker at lunch." Maggie appeared calm, but a lump was forming in the pit of her stomach. Her friends exchanged another look, but they both nodded in agreement.

With little more conversation, they finished eating and headed to class. The schedule for the day was always the same. They had classes until 3:00 pm, then an hour of physical fitness, two hours of chores – to help reduce the cost of running the center – followed by dinner, studying, and sleep. Maggie and Jules spent their entire day together, which eased the repetitiveness.

But where the monotony was normally almost relaxing, over the next two days, it filled her with dread. Ryker had still not returned, and Maggie's imagination ran wild with possibilities of what had happened to him. There was nothing to distract her from her own thoughts.

"He hasn't come back to the room at all," Luke said as he sat down to breakfast on the morning of the third day.

Maggie's stomach twisted, and the food in front of her was suddenly nauseating. "You have to be kidding. Have you seen him at all?"

He shook his head.

"I'm sure there's an explanation," Jules said.

"That doesn't mean it's a good one," Maggie said.

"You're as bad as him." She rolled her eyes. "Name one reason you think something awful has happened.

Better yet, name one time when something awful has happened before."

"How about us being stuck in here? Being taken away from our parents?" Luke said.

"You barely even remember your parents. I'd be willing to bet most of what you think you remember is just your imagination at this point." Jules spoke matter-of-factly.

"You have no right—"

"Enough!" Maggie was sick of listening to their argument. It happened too often to count. Jules had spent so much of her life at Jessup, she didn't know anything else, and after having listened to DRM approved lessons for so long, she truly believed the Reproduction Act was not only necessary, but also good.

According to their teachers, the law was first enacted in an attempt to stem the violence and neglect plaguing America's children. By only allowing qualified people to have children, violence would decrease, while educational and housing standards would increase. In theory, it made perfect sense. Having no memory of the outside world herself, Maggie understood why Jules believed it, but she'd experienced too much to agree. "All I'm going to say is, Ms. Larson."

Jules looked at her and nodded. "Ok, there's one. Though I maintain, we don't know the entire story there."

"Maybe Ryker's been sent to the advanced center."

Luke shoveled food into his mouth as he spoke, and Maggie's stomach turned again.

"He's only 17. He has another year," Jules said.

At the age of 18, each child was sent to one of two types of advanced centers. One merely prepared students for adulthood and living on their own. The other taught highly focused courses, preparing students for careers with the DRM.

Maggie knew Jules was right, but it didn't ease her growing anxiety. What if they sent him a year early? She stood up without having eaten one bite of food.

"Where are you going?"

"I'm sick of guessing. I'm going to talk to Mr. Jacobs."

Luke laughed. "He's not going to tell you the truth."

"He's a nice guy. If I can talk to him one-on-one, I bet he will." Maggie had always liked Mr. Jacobs. She often thought that if he were more involved in the day-to-day function of the center, it wouldn't be such a terrible place to live. Unfortunately, that task was left to Captain Hayden, a man who prided himself on strict rule enforcement. And although Mr. Jacobs was in charge of the center, Hayden didn't answer to him. He reported directly to the DRM, which really meant he answered to no one.

Maggie left the cafeteria, glancing to make sure no Remos were looking her way. Luckily, they were all distracted by their own conversations. She moved quickly through the halls, but as she rounded the last corner and the offices came into view, she ran directly into Hayden.

"What are you doing? You should be at breakfast." His voice was stern, as it always was. He was dressed in the Remos uniform – black pants and jacket, a thick belt holding a number of unidentifiable tools, and large, black boots. Although this was all standard, he somehow looked more frightening than the others. He towered above most of the students, and adding his dark hair and cold eyes, his demeanor was intimidating. For some reason, he'd always had a particular dislike for Maggie.

"I need to speak with Mr. Jacobs."

"You need to return to the cafeteria."

"I will, as soon as I speak with him." She tried to step around, but he grabbed her shirt and pulled her back in front of him.

"What did I just say?" His voice grew louder.

"It's important."

He laughed but released his grip. "All right, what is it you need to speak with him about?"

She shifted on her feet, glancing from Hayden to the floor. "My brother has been gone for the last few days, and I want to know what happened to him."

A dark smile spread across his face. "You don't know?"

"Know what?"

"Big brother is being tested to determine his aptitude

for a career in the DRM. From what I hear, he is being well received by Uptown." Uptown was the closest advanced center to Jessup. It was rumored to turn its students into Remos, often against their will.

She shook her head. "He's too young for an advanced center. Besides, he would never work for them."

"Testing is done early for processing purposes, and which advanced center he is sent to isn't his choice. Now you have your answer. Get back to the cafeteria."

Maggie's stomach twisted again. She didn't trust Hayden, but what he was saying made too much sense. She had to confirm with Mr. Jacobs. "Thank you for your help, but I'd still like to speak with Mr. Jacobs." The firmness of her voice surprised even her. She stepped around him, but only made it two steps before his hand clamped down on her shirt once again.

His eyes narrowed. "Obviously, you need help finding your way back. Allow me to assist you."

Chapter Three

The rest of the day went by in a blur. Maggie couldn't tell Jules what Hayden had said. To say it aloud was too much like agreeing with it, and regardless, she knew Jules would see becoming a Remo as more of an honor than a curse. But if Ryker were sent to Uptown, she knew she'd never see him again. Worst yet, he'd become one of them.

For the first time in a while, Ms. Larson consumed her thoughts. She had been a teacher at Jessup and the closest thing to a mother that Maggie had ever known. Still, ever since she left, Maggie had tried hard to forget her. Remembering was too painful, but it was impossible to forget. She often thought of their first real conversation together.

"Me and Jules decided we don't want to have kids. It's such a waste of time and it just sounds awful," Maggie had said. Ms. Larson used to pull her off chore duty so they could spend time alone together. She called it tutoring, but they never discussed material from class.

"Don't say that. Having kids is wonderful." Ms. Larson smiled. Her gray hair and wrinkling features somehow couldn't overshadow her youthful grin and lively eyes.

"You don't have any." Tears came to her teacher's eyes, and even at twelve, Maggie could see she'd upset her. "I'm sorry, I didn't think you did."

"I have you." She shook her head, but her smile never wavered.

"I don't count." Maggie laughed, though she felt warmth in her chest.

"And why not? I've taken care of you since the day you arrived here. You were the tiniest little baby, but you could cry so loud." Ms. Larson laughed.

"A baby? Babies don't come here. I must've been three or four. Even still, you're not really convincing me to have kids if they just sit around crying all the time."

Ms. Larson's face suddenly turned serious. For a moment, she just stared at Maggie before glancing cautiously around the room. She pulled a small device from her pocket and held it tightly in her hands.

"What is that?" Maggie asked.

"It's a jamming device."

She leaned forward to get a better look. It was round and smaller than a cell phone but nearly twice as thick. A green light ran around the circumference of the device and she could see a singular switch on top. Maggie had never seen one in real life before, but she'd heard how people would use them to interfere with DRM surveillance equipment. "Those are illegal. Criminals use those to avoid being arrested." Maggie paused. "Why do you have one?"

Ms. Larson hesitated, turning the device over in her hands, and then exhaled. She flipped the small switch and the green light instantly transformed into red.

"Everything they've taught you here is a lie. Your parents are not criminals, they're not evil people. They just wanted a family. The DRM was started by those that want to control what kinds of people can have kids. It has nothing to do with the best interests of the nation."

"But my parents are criminals, they broke the law. And some people shouldn't have kids. They'll just let terrible things happen to them and not care for them properly."

Ms. Larson took her hands and held them gently. "You think that's true of everyone that's denied a permit?"

"Of course."

She nodded, but her grip tightened softly on Maggie's hands. "I was denied a permit. Would you think of me as an unfit mother? Have I inflicted terrible things upon you?" Her voice broke faintly.

Guilt seized Maggie. "No! You're fantastic. Why would they say no to you?"

"After my husband died, they said a child shouldn't

be raised in a single parent home. I petitioned to take custody of you when you first arrived at Jessup. This was no place for a baby. Even after everything I did to prove I would be a fit mother, they still said no."

Maggie looked at the ground and thought of how different her life would have been if she had been adopted. She'd be without her brother and her friends, but still, a part of her felt the sting of a lost normal childhood. "You keep saying baby. What do you mean? They don't allow them here."

Ms. Larson paused. "You're different…special. I just want you to remember that here at Jessup you learn what they want you to learn. They're trying so hard to erase any trace of you before this place, any trace of your family, and if you let them, they'll succeed."

"So, my parents, they're not bad people?" It had gone against everything she'd ever learned, but coming from Ms. Larson, she knew it was the truth.

"If their only crime in the world was loving you, would you call them bad?"

Maggie shook her head, trying to force the conversation from her mind. She knew it would eventually lead to their final moments together, which was something she couldn't stand to remember. Especially when she was already so anxious about her brother. By the time dinner finally came around, she feared any food that went into her stomach would simply come back up.

"Hey look, it's Ryker," Jules said as they exited the food line with their trays.

Maggie saw him sitting at their normal table. It always amazed her how different the two of them looked, especially since they were only a year apart. She had bright blue eyes, long dark brown hair, and stood at only 5'4". He, on the other hand, had army cropped, light brown hair, gray eyes, and was over 6 feet tall. Adding in his broad shoulders, he held much more of a presence than she did.

"Thank God you're all right." Maggie sat down across from him and only then saw how pale he was. Dark circles sat heavy under his eyes.

Ryker smiled. "I'm fine."

"Where have you been?"

"They took me for testing." Her stomach tightened. "They said it was for college scholarships, but I knew it was for the DRM. Don't look so worried. I performed miserably. According to their test, I'm neither smart nor athletic."

"So, they don't want you?"

"No, they said I'm not the right material."

"Of course you're not. I'm amazed you can tie your shoes in the morning." Luke laughed.

"Maggie, you shouldn't—" Ryker stopped. He was no longer looking at her but passed her.

She turned around to see Hayden standing right behind them.

"Welcome back, Mr. Ward. How was the test?"

"Unfortunately, I don't think I'm what they're looking for," Ryker said, amusement hanging on every word.

"Oh, that's too bad." The same tone was in Hayden's voice. "I'm sure you did your best though."

"Of course."

Hayden glanced at Maggie and winked. Her heart stopped. "Well, I know Ms. Ward is happy to see you back. Enjoy your dinner."

She merely nodded. She knew the look on Hayden's face well. It was the same one she got every time he caught her doing something wrong. It was satisfaction. Ryker was in danger.

"So, what was the testing like?" Jules asked.

"Two parts to it. A written test and then a physical test. The physical part would've been fun if it had been for any other reason. It was your standard timed run, push-ups and sit-ups, but then they had an obstacle course to see who could get through it the fastest and quietest."

"The quietest?" Luke said. "Yeah, that seems like a normal requirement for a college scholarship."

"I know. As soon as they said that, it was a dead giveaway."

"But that was after you already did the rest of the test?"

"Yeah, the first part was the written exam, but don't worry. They told us who had been disqualified as we were leaving."

"How many were accepted?" Jules was relaxed, eating her food as if it were any other dinner.

"Two guys. They weren't from Jessup. I think they were both 18, so it makes more sense."

They continued talking, but Maggie wasn't listening. Hayden's words repeated over and over and she couldn't stop picturing his knowing smile. Deep down, she knew what was happening, but she didn't want to believe it. If Hayden was right, they would keep Ryker at Jessup for another year, and then ship him to Uptown the moment he turned 18. Her stomach turned.

The only way to know for sure was to read Ryker's personal file. Unfortunately, the only way to read that file was to break into Mr. Jacob's office. She glanced at Ryker, who would never approve of such a risk, and immediately knew one thing. She couldn't tell him until after the job was already done.

Chapter Four

Maggie had previously broken into Mr. Jacobs' office on two occasions, but both times she had been nervous. It was one of the most difficult places to get to and she knew this was because of the valuable information located within. Unlike her previous trips, which were taken for amusement, this was serious.

If she could find out the truth about her brother's test, there was a chance they'd be able to get his acceptance reconsidered. All it would take was a drastic drop in his grades or his physical performance. But to do this without the right information would mean ruining his chances of college and a better life. Maggie shook her head. She needed to focus.

She slipped out of her room, careful not to wake anyone up. Although she desperately wanted to tell Jules, she knew her friend would try to talk her out of it. In order to get to the office, she had to first get to the gymnasium. It was just down the hall from the administrative offices and was one of two places in the building where the vents were large enough to fit into.

The Remos that monitored the center at night were known for their ability to move silently through the halls, making it impossible to know where they were at any particular time. Maggie made her way slowly, careful to move as quietly as possible. Adrenaline pumped through her body, but for the first time in days, she felt more herself than ever. She was no longer just sitting on the sidelines waiting for news.

Once safely inside the gymnasium, she exhaled. The hardest part was over. She went to the far corner and used the bleachers to reach the vent. The screws were loose from previous excursions, making it possible to get them off quickly. She slid the grate behind the bleachers and lifted herself up.

The vent was a tight fit, forcing Maggie to crawl. The metal creaked and popped as she went, and she feared the noise could be heard in the hallway below. In her mind, she repeated the turns: right, left, right, right. Finally, she arrived at the grate that led directly into the administrative offices and unscrewed the vent from the inside, though it was painful to force her fingers to grab them in such an awkward way.

She left the bottom screw in place, allowing the grate to swing down and out of the way. As quietly as possible, Maggie lowered herself into the office. There was only silence. She smiled. Mr. Jacobs' door was always locked, but she knew where the spare key was in the secretary's desk. She grabbed it, and in seconds, she was secluded in Mr. Jacobs' office. She immediately went to the filing cabinet and found Ryker's file.

Maggie brought the file to Mr. Jacobs' desk and turned on the lamp. All the information matched what she'd previously read, that is until she got to the last page. There was a new entry.

Uptown Test Results:

Ward, Ryker

Physical aptitude – 98%
Academic percentile – 97%

Based on the subject's high marks in both the physical and academic examinations, RYKER WARD is approved for placement at the Uptown Advanced Reeducation Center. The American Testing Council unanimously agrees that the subject's temperament and propensity for sympathy toward illegals will not be a factor once his education at Uptown is complete. Subject is to be informed of his acceptance on his 18th birthday.

Final Status: ACCEPTED

Maggie's hands flew to the desk to steady her balance. Her fingers shook against the wood as she sat down in Mr. Jacobs' chair and reread the report once again. They were going to send him away to become a Remo, and worst of all, they had no doubt they could. She thought of all the Remos that worked at the center and imagined the ones that had ripped her family apart. Never had she heard a story of a good Remo, and in her heart, she knew that if Ryker went to Uptown, he would not be the exception.

She closed the file, replacing it once again in its proper place. Pushing the drawer shut, she didn't pay attention and it slammed loudly. Her heart stopped as the noise vibrated off the walls. It was time to go. She hurriedly turned the light off and opened the office door. There stood Hayden.

His eyes widened in surprise as he stared at her. Neither of them moved nor spoke. She glanced at the open door behind him and thought about running, but she knew it wouldn't do any good. He knew who she was.

"What are you doing in here?" he demanded. He glanced back to the door. He was searching for how she gained entrance until his eyes finally settled on the open vent cover.

"Sleepwalking." She'd been caught out at night before but never in a truly restricted place.

"Don't get smart. What are you doing in here?" he

yelled.

"Nothing," she said quickly. "I guess I'm on extra chores for a week. Understandable, I'll just head back to my room."

She tried to maneuver passed him, but he grabbed her shoulder painfully hard.

"Not this time." He dragged her passed Mr. Jacobs' office into his own. Maggie had been in Hayden's office on more than one occasion, and each time she wanted to leave as quickly as possible. "Now, how did you get into his office? Obviously, you made your way here through the vents. Clever. But I know he keeps his door locked."

Maggie glanced around the room, searching for the best answer.

"Answer me!"

"I used a key." She slipped it out of her pocket and onto his desk, figuring honesty was the best play.

Hayden's eyes narrowed. "Stealing is against policy, but so is sneaking around the halls after hours, breaking into the administrative offices and reading files that don't belong to you."

"So, if I tell you I was reading my own file, that would be ok?" She said before she could stop herself.

"Enough! I've put up with you for too long. You have been warned several times, and yet you never seem to learn."

Maggie shook her head. "No, I did."

"You just chose to ignore them?"

"No, it's not like that. I just, um, didn't think. I know it wasn't the right thing to do. I'm prepared to accept my punishment, extra chores or whatever."

"As I said, we're beyond that. You've consistently and deliberately broken this same rule time and time again. Now, we've progressed from wandering the halls, to breaking in and entering a restricted area. Even stealing a key to do so. You knew exactly what you were doing, and you're going to tell me why you are here."

Maggie's heart raced. This wasn't his normal reaction and she was afraid. "All right. I wanted to find out if you were telling me the truth about Ryker. I needed to know what his test results were."

Hayden smiled. "And did it confirm what I said?"

"Yes, but that's not what he told me." She looked to her feet, no longer wanting to see the self-satisfied grin on his face.

"Of course he didn't. He doesn't know." He sat down at his desk and stared at her. She shifted on her feet, not sure where to look. Everywhere was uncomfortable. "I was going to transfer you. That was my intent when I brought you in here."

Maggie's heart stopped. "Transfer? To where?"

"The Skeel High Security Center." Panic pulsed in her chest. The high security centers were said to be worse than even the advanced centers. The kids that were sent there were ferial. They grew up underground, on the streets.

She was certain she wouldn't survive being thrown in with them. And the Remos there were said to be some of the harshest in the country. "But now I'm wondering if it wouldn't be a more fitting punishment just to leave you here all alone. I'm sure I could get big brother's transfer moved up. He could be the youngest person to attend Uptown and spend two full years there."

"No. Please don't do that. Transfer me." She nodded insistently.

Hayden's smile grew darker as he shook his head. "As I said, this is much more fitting. It will teach you that your actions not only affect you but also those around you.

"But—"

"This is not up for discussion. Now we can get you back to your room."

Her mind was still spinning as Hayden jerked her from the room. The feeling of nausea did not go away, instead, it steadily grew stronger. If Ryker spent an extra year at Uptown, he'd have no chance to avoid brainwashing. It was so effective at Jessup that if it hadn't been for Ms. Larson, she would've succumbed long ago. How much worse would it be at Uptown? Bile rose to her mouth, but she pushed it back down. She would not give Hayden the satisfaction. They rounded another corner and he jerked her sharply.

"You know, I can walk on my own," Maggie snapped.

"It is what got you here in the first place." He smiled

but did not release her.

"You really do enjoy ruining people's lives. No wonder you work for the DRM. You're all alike."

"That we are. Now you know what big brother will be like in a few short years."

"That's not true. He will never be like you."

He laughed. "Oh no, he won't be like me. From your perspective, he'll be worse. He'll be a machine that does what it's told, and only what it's told. Which, in this case, means hunting down people like you."

Without thinking, she stomped on his foot and tried to yank her shirt free, but he had an iron clasp. Hayden pushed her against the wall and used his forearm to lock her in place.

"You need to learn to keep that temper under control." Hayden was inches from her face. His voice was quiet and menacing and sent shivers down her spine. "Don't you realize what path you and Ryker are now on?"

"What path is that?" Rage like she'd never felt seethed through her.

He smiled. "Years from now, Ryker will be a well-trained officer, and you, most likely, will be a criminal." Her stomach tightened as she realized what he was going to say next. "Your paths will cross again with big brother arresting you and bringing your own illegals right back here."

Chapter Five

"Maggie, you haven't said two words all morning." Jules punched her in the arm, jolting her out of her deep thoughts.

She glanced around, only then realizing they were in line at the cafeteria. Her mind had been working all night, and she hadn't slept. The reality of what happened had settled in and left her desperately searching for a solution. Maggie looked to their table and was relieved to see Ryker and Luke waiting.

"What's wrong?" Ryker asked as they sat down.

"I did something. I didn't mean for it to go the way it did, honestly. I was trying to help." The lack of sleep was making it difficult to form complete sentences.

"Tell me what happened." He said in what Maggie always referred to as his "big brother voice", which he only used when he was mad. She didn't answer right away. "Hayden caught you doing something again, didn't he?"

"Yes." She explained everything that had happened. Ryker tried to interrupt multiple times but she talked over him, ignoring the incredulous looks coming from Jules and Luke.

"Are they really going to send me to Uptown?" His voice was barely above a whisper.

Maggie nodded. "It's my fault too."

"He would've been sent eventually anyway," Jules said.

Ryker shook his head. "Jules is right." His face grew paler by the second, and though he was looking at the table, Maggie could see the fear growing in his eyes.

"It's going to be ok. I'm not going to let them send you away," she said.

"There's nothing that can be done about it."

"No, I have a plan."

"Let it go." Ryker's voice strained.

"Ryker, we can—"

"I said let it go!" he yelled.

"Keep your voice down," Luke said as several Remos looked their way.

Ryker rubbed his temple and took a deep breath. "I'm sorry, but the last thing I need right now is any hope that I'll avoid this. I just need to accept it."

"But there is hope—"

"What, may I ask, makes you think shouting is suddenly acceptable?" Hayden interrupted. All four of them looked up, startled by his sudden appearance.

"Nothing, sorry," Ryker said.

Hayden looked from him to Maggie and smiled. "Just heard the news, did we? Only this morning, Mr. Jacobs approved your early transfer. You should be proud. The first from this center."

"That actually is exciting," Jules said. For the first time, their differing opinions on the DRM felt like an insurmountable trench, and Maggie couldn't help but feel betrayed by her friend.

"Real exciting," Ryker mumbled.

"And there's no need to worry about leaving Jessup. Within a few weeks, you won't even remember it."

He looked from Maggie to Hayden and his eyes narrowed. "What do you mean?"

"Oh, they have miraculous ways of helping their students to focus, one of which is helping them to forget their lives before enrollment." The cheer in his voice flamed the anger in Maggie's chest.

"That won't happen to him," she said through clenched teeth.

"Of course not." Hayden looked at his watch. "You children should finish up, breakfast is nearly over."

They watched him walk away, but Maggie could feel as everyone's gaze shifted back to her brother. Anger was gone, replaced by concern and fear.

"I could be gone by the end of the week."

"But not to Uptown." Maggie shook her head. "We're going to escape."

Luke laughed. "No one has ever escaped from here."

"That's because there's no need to. Hayden just said all that to mess with you. I bet Uptown is fine. You guys need to calm down." Jules scraped the last bit of food from her plate. She looked appraisingly at Maggie's untouched plate and grabbed her piece of toast.

"Are you serious?" They shared each other's food all the time, but in that moment, she wanted to snatch the toast from her hand. "We know for a fact that everything they've taught us here is a lie. Ms. Larson—"

"Oh God, don't bring that up again. She was an old lady that was losing it. I'm not trying to be mean, but let's be honest."

Maggie grinded her teeth hard but forced herself to take a deep breath and calm down. Arguing with Jules was not the pressing concern. She turned back to Ryker. "No one would expect an escape. I know this center better than anyone, especially at night. We can do this." She searched her brother's face for an answer, but after several seconds, he shook his head.

"No. If they caught us, you'd be sent to a high security center. I won't risk that."

"That's not up to you."

"I'm not going to allow both of our futures to be ruined."

"I was nearly transferred anyway, so I'm already at risk."

"But you weren't transferred. I was." Ryker stood

abruptly. He hesitated for a moment before leaving the cafeteria without another word. Luke shrugged uncomfortably and followed him.

Maggie and Jules sat in silence.

"We need to get to class," Jules said finally.

It was impossible to focus. Maggie searched for a way to convince her brother. She knew if she were facing an inevitable transfer, he would be on board, but this left her with only one viable option. And it wasn't one she was thrilled about. She wrote down the entirety of the plan, step by step, and by the time the lunch bell rang, her heart was racing.

Ryker was even paler than he'd been at breakfast. He pushed his food around the plate but made no attempt to eat. Maggie took a deep breath before speaking.

"Have you given any more thought to the escape?"

"No. I'm not going to do that." He didn't look up.

"You could go on your own."

Ryker shook his head.

"Would you stop sulking and come up with a solution then?" She would not allow him to resign to such a fate.

"You're the only one that knows this place well enough to get us out. If I tried on my own, I'd be done for, and I'm not going to let you risk getting caught for me. So I'm not really left with much else," Ryker snapped.

"I could break your leg." Luke snapped the carrot he was eating with a loud crack. "Then they wouldn't want you."

"That's stupid," Jules had said little since breakfast, and Maggie knew she was actively trying to avoid the fight that was sitting just under the surface.

Maggie rolled her eyes. "For goodness sake, Ryker—"

"Just leave it alone!" He slammed his fist on the table and their plates shook noisily against the wood. Before any Remos could respond, he stood and left the table.

Fear began growing in her stomach as she realized what had to be done. She took a deep breath and glanced around the cafeteria. Hayden was watching them from across the room. She looked back to Jules.

"I need you to get this to Ryker." She slid a folded paper across the table.

"What is it?"

"Instructions on how to escape."

"He won't go without you, so please just let it go. It's really not that big of a deal."

"Just promise me you will make sure he gets this." Maggie looked back to Hayden. He was still there. When she didn't answer, she pushed the paper closer to Jules so that it was sitting just in front of her.

Jules grinded her teeth but nodded. Maggie took another deep breath, trying to calm her nerves. Before she could talk herself down, she stood up, grabbed her uneaten tray of food, and walked across the cafeteria to where Hayden stood. *Breathe.*

"Good afternoon, Ms. Ward. I'm sad to see your

brother doesn't look in good spirits." Hayden's smug grin returned to his face.

"You could change that." She was surprised by the strength in her voice. She felt so nervous.

"I am. As I said, in a few weeks he'll be just fine. Better even." He laughed. "Really, you should be thanking—"

With all her strength, Maggie slammed the tray of food into Hayden's face, sending forceful vibrations through her arms. He flew backward to the floor as blood gushed everywhere. The students gasped as all eyes locked on her and she could hear the Remos shouting and running toward her. She tensed her body just as one of them slammed against her, knocking her roughly to the ground. His knee pushed into her spine as he pulled her arms back and cinched them together.

They jerked her to her feet right as Hayden regained his balance. Some of the other Remos asked him if he needed a doctor, but he growled at them to be quiet. He grabbed her shirt and yanked her forcefully from the cafeteria. Maggie had difficulty keeping up with his fast pace and her bound hands made it hard to keep her balance. They burst into the administrative office and she tripped over her own feet, but his grip on her shirt kept her upright.

"What is this?" Mr. Jacobs had come out of his office right as they tried to pass.

"I'm dealing with it," Hayden said.

"I hit him with a cafeteria tray," Maggie said. "In the

face."

Mr. Jacobs leaned in closer to inspect the damage. He was in awe. "She did this?"

"Yes," Hayden grumbled. "As I said, I'm dealing with it."

"You should get yourself cleaned up and I'll fill out the transfer paperwork."

"Transfer?" Hayden's grip on her shoulder tightened unexpectedly. "I'm not transferring her."

"You have no choice. It's DRM policy. Any child that physically assaults a staff member must be immediately transferred to the nearest high security center. There is zero tolerance." Mr. Jacobs was firm.

"That would be a reprieve considering what I plan to do to her," Hayden said. Maggie's heart was racing. "No one needs to know what happened."

"Captain, not only was this incident witnessed by most of the student and staff population, but we would be going against the oaths we took when joining the DRM to ignore such a blatant display. I understand that you're upset, but that is the policy. Now, you go get cleaned up while I begin the process."

They held each other's stare for several seconds, neither man wanting to back down. Finally, Hayden released his grip on Maggie and left the office. She smirked.

"I'd wipe that smile off your face. By this time tomorrow, you'll be living with some of the worst offenders in the state. You'll be wishing I had listened to Captain Hayden."

Mr. Jacobs led her down the hall, passed Hayden's office, to the most dreaded place in the entire building. Maggie took a deep breath as he opened the holding room door. Really, it was the center's prison. It was a small room with cement walls and floor. A single metal bed sat in one corner and a toilet in the other. That was it.

"You'll remain here until tomorrow when the transport will take you to Skeel." Nothing more was said as the door was locked shut.

Maggie sat on the edge of the stiff and uncomfortable bed. Jules would deliver the letter and it would all be fine. Her note outlined to Ryker what had happened to her, where she was, and how he could get her out. Neither of them had anything to lose now and she knew that would propel him to act. Even if he was caught, they'd still send him to Uptown to train the rebelliousness out of him, but she had faith in her brother. Maggie lay down and closed her eyes. In a few hours, they would leave Jessup forever, together.

Chapter Six

Maggie paced back and forth in the cramped room. Four steps one way, then four the other. She could feel it was getting late, though no one had come to see her since Mr. Jacobs locked the door in place. At first, she tried to sleep but quickly realized her anxiety would not allow it. Instead, she inspected every inch of the room and found a vent located just under the bed, although it was too small to fit through. If Ryker didn't make it to her, the transfer would be inevitable.

When the frustration of pacing finally got to her, she sat on the floor and leaned against the door. She closed her eyes and, immediately, Ms. Larson came to mind. *Is this where they brought her that day?*

It remained burned in her memory, the day she finally understood the reality of the DRM. After Ms. Larson had first told her the truth, they continued to talk for weeks about the act and how it really worked.

Maggie listened day after day as Ms. Larson told her about families being torn apart, children being put in prison for disagreeing with the government, and how children's names were changed to make it more difficult for illegal families to reunite even after sentences were served. With each story, Maggie began to realize she'd been tricked into believing lies.

Then that day happened. They were sitting in her classroom with the jamming device on the table between them.

"I've told Jules a lot of what we talked about. She thinks I'm making it up," Maggie had said. She had argued with Jules a lot, and she liked having someone to talk to.

"She was four when she came here. She doesn't remember anything else."

"I was a baby, that doesn't mean I can't understand the truth." She didn't want to tell Ms. Larson that in her arguments with Jules, she often saw her friend's point and wondered if her teacher was right.

Ms. Larson smiled. "She'll come around. I brought you another book." She pulled a ragged paperback out of her drawer.

Maggie laughed as she picked it up. No one ever used real books anymore. Everything was done electronically. "Where do you even find these things?"

"It's not some ancient artifact. People still read books," Ms. Larson said with a laugh.

"Not like this." She flipped through the pages. "What's it about?"

"The early years of the DRM. The truth about how the program was implemented in the start. I thought this might help you better understand the history." She put her hand on the book, bringing Maggie's eyes to hers. "I'll keep it here in my desk and you can read it during our time together."

She nodded and looked back down at the book. "If this is from 2055, why is it a paper book?"

"The government monitors all electronic books. This was banned shortly after the DRM expanded and the only way to get it out was through hard copies."

"That's smart, using such an old-school method."

Ms. Larson laughed. "It's not that old-school."

The door burst open, sending shards of wood through the air. In seconds, the space was swarmed by Remos circling through the room and preventing either of them from moving. From the door, Hayden walked toward them slowly and shook his head.

"What have we here?" His eyes went from Maggie to Ms. Larson and fell finally on the jamming device between them. He picked it up. "And what is it we don't want anyone to hear?"

"Maggie should return to class." Ms. Larson sat up straight and Maggie smiled at the teacher's lack of fear.

Hayden snatched the book from Maggie's hands. His jaw tightened as he read the title. "Did you read this?"

She tried to take it back, but he moved it away too quickly. "That's mine."

"Did you read this?" he demanded. When she didn't answer, he grabbed her arm and yanked her out of the chair. "Answer me."

She shook her head. "No."

He stared hard at her for a moment before putting the book in his front pocket and shoving her toward another Remo. "Take her to class. Ms. Larson, you'll need to come with us."

She walked to Maggie and pulled the girl into her arms. "Remember everything I've told you. Stay safe," she whispered hurriedly. "I love you."

Hayden jerked them apart.

"Wait, where are they taking you? When will you be back?" Maggie's heart raced as she fully realized the gravity of the situation.

"She won't be back." Hayden pushed Ms. Larson to two nearby Remos, who immediately handcuffed her hands behind her back.

Maggie tried to stop them, but the Remo behind her held a tight grip on her shirt. Tears streamed down her face as she helplessly watched them pull her teacher from the room.

"Ms. Larson! You can't do this! She didn't do anything wrong!" Maggie shouted.

"This is what happens to people that break the law," Hayden said. "Remember that."

It was in that moment that she knew everything Ms. Larson had told her was true. It was also the last time she ever saw her. Maggie swallowed hard as the memory danced in her mind and she wondered once again if this was the same place they'd brought Ms. Larson that day.

The sound of sharp scratching startled her back to the present. She put her ear against the door and followed the noise to the lock. Someone was trying to open it. Maggie's heart fluttered with excitement, knowing it must be Ryker. But just as quickly as it started, the noise stopped. She strained to hear more and pressed as tightly against the door as possible. Silence. Then it happened. The clear sound of a key going into a lock.

Maggie pushed herself away from the door, barely giving it enough room to swing inward. She smiled eagerly as the handle turned and the door opened, but her stomach dropped as Hayden stepped into the light.

"It doesn't matter who you are. You didn't really think I'd let you leave without answering for this, did you?" He pointed at his nose, which had swollen twice its normal size.

"I hadn't really thought about it." It was the truth.

His eyes narrowed as he stepped toward her. Fear jolted through her body. Maggie knew she had to run, every instinct screamed at her to get out of the room. She sprinted right at him, hoping to knock him to the ground, but he grabbed her left arm and twisted it painfully behind her. She stomped on his foot. He grunted angrily and whipped her around, throwing her to the floor. She kicked at his legs, but he knelt on top of her. He smiled as he raised his hand up. She tried to protect her face, but he pushed her arm out of the way.

Just as the strike was about to fall, Ryker emerged from the hallway and tackled him off of her. He punched Hayden over and over, each blow echoing sickly in the small space. For the first time, Maggie realized just how large her brother was. Hayden struggled to get out from underneath him, but from his position, Ryker had him trapped. After a short struggle, he grabbed Hayden's head and slammed his face against the floor. A loud crack vibrated through the room, followed by a deafening silence. Hayden was absolutely still.

"Did you kill him?" The thought brought bile to her throat. She hated the man, but even so, never would she want her brother to do such a thing. To be capable of such a thing.

Ryker looked up at her as sweat dripped down his face. He shook his head. "No, he's only knocked out. We have to go."

Maggie nodded and happily left the cement room. A figure appeared in front of her and she swung with all her strength. There was no going back now. Her fist slammed into her opponent and sent them to the ground.

"Maggie, it's me!" Jules yelled.

She squinted in the darkness and could just make

out her friend's familiar features. "Oh my God, what are you doing here?"

Jules stood up while rubbing her cheek. "Really? No apology?"

"We don't have time for this. Come on." Ryker moved to the main door that led into the administrative office. Luke stood there waiting.

"You didn't think you'd leave me behind, did you?" He smiled.

"You guys are coming with us?" She couldn't believe they would take the risk when they didn't have to.

Jules shifted uncomfortably. "I came to talk you out of this."

"You're kidding me," Ryker said. "We don't have time for this."

The desperation in Jules' eyes made it impossible for Maggie to feel angry. She shook her head. "I'm sorry, but we have to go."

"There's no life out there. How are you going to survive on the run?" Jules grabbed her hands. "The high security centers can't be that bad. They're just schools. You have to see that."

"All I see is hundreds of government-made orphans." Maggie hugged her and whispered, "I hope we see each other again."

She pulled away before Jules could protest and followed Ryker and Luke into the hallway. Jules followed nonetheless, but when she opened her mouth to speak,

Ryker held up his finger, telling them to be quiet. Maggie led the way, knowing the shortest route to their destination: the math hallway, at the end of which stood a door that led out of the building. It was the exit closest to the massive tree line that surrounded the center. Suddenly, all the lights in the hallway came blindingly on. Her heart leapt to her throat as a loud alarm blared, echoing down the halls.

"They know!" Ryker yelled. "Come on!"

They followed him, running through the halls as fast as they could. Luke got to the end of the math hall first but stopped just short of the double doors. They all froze in front of them, knowing they were seconds from freedom.

"Make a run for the trees. No matter what, don't stop," Ryker instructed.

"Maggie, this is your last chance. Please don't do this," Jules begged.

"If you hide in one of the classrooms, you should be able to sneak back to the room before they realize you're gone." She looked from her friend to her brother and nodded.

Luke and Ryker pushed the doors open, but before they could move, another siren rang as a thick, metal door shot down from the top of the doorway. Maggie shoved Ryker out of the way, knocking him and Jules outside. The door missed them by inches, but as Luke tried to move clear, it slammed down and caught his leg in its grasp. He screamed in pain.

Maggie threw herself to the floor and could see Ryker on the other side looking back at her.

"Can you fit underneath?"

"No, it's too small." The door was being held open by Luke's leg. "Just go. I'll find another way out."

"No." Ryker grabbed the edge and pulled upward, but it only raised an inch. Luke screamed as the relief of pressure sent more pain down his leg. Knowing what had to be done, she seized the opportunity and shoved Luke's leg out of the way. "Maggie, no!"

The door slipped from his hands and slammed shut, sealing her alone inside.

+ + +

She wasted no time. Maggie ran from the door, searching for another that was still open, but each hall she turned down was blocked. Panic began to set in. She needed a way out. She ordered her brain to think. The siren continued to echo through the halls, reminding her of the vibrating echo of the vents. *The vents.* There were two she could fit in but only one that might help.

Maggie sprinted toward the kitchen. She could hear heavy footsteps, accompanied by shouting. Remos were mobilizing and they were on the hunt. She slowed her movement, taking time to check around corners before proceeding. Still, the slower she moved, the faster her heart raced.

The kitchen vent she needed was located on the floor near the stove. She pried it off with a long steel skewer, no longer caring about any damage she might do. Once inside, she followed the cramped venting up, knowing it should lead to the roof. Inch by inch, she crawled until she finally reached the end of the dark tunnel, only to find that she wasn't on the roof. Looking through the small grate, she realized she was on the side of the building. Maggie took a deep breath.

She kicked the grate over and over until it flew off. As carefully as possible, she lowered herself out of the opening and let go. Dropping ten feet, she crashed painfully to the ground. Every muscle ached as she stood, but she smiled when she saw the woods only thirty feet away. Voices rang out nearby. Remos were coming for her.

Too afraid to look back, she ran. As she made her way into the woods, her speed slowed. The terrain was rocky and uneven, and along with the slippery leaves, it made it difficult for her to keep her footing. Still, she pressed on. Without warning, she was jerked to the ground right as something whizzed by. The Remos were shooting at her. The fear of being shot had momentarily dulled Maggie to the body beside her, but as a hand cinched around her wrist, she opened her mouth to scream.

A second hand clamped down on her lips,

containing the sound inside. Maggie struggled against the restraints, but as her eyes adjusted, she made out Ryker's face. She threw her arms around him.

"Follow me," he whispered.

Ryker crawled along the forest floor, moving perpendicular to the center behind them. Maggie followed as carefully as she could, but she felt twigs breaking under her body and feared she would give them away. Remos shouted. Their voices were getting closer, forcing more adrenaline to surge through her body. Every instinct told her to run, but she forced herself to follow Ryker's methodical movements. He stopped but waved her forward to him.

"We're going to wait for them to pass us, then double back," he whispered.

She shook her head. "They'll see us for sure."

"Crawl under that bush behind you. Trust me."

She held his gaze for a moment and then did as he instructed. The bush was thick and prickly, but large. She clawed her way underneath and found the dirt considerably wetter than the rest of the ground. As she lay there, the cold muck began soaking through her clothes, sending shivers down her spine. Ryker crawled a few feet away to the crux of a large tree. He tried to nestle tightly against it, but she could still see him. Maggie opened her mouth to reiterate that this would not work, but she froze when a branch cracked behind her. Remos were there. Next to them. Her heart stopped.

"You're sure you saw them go this way?" It was Hayden. She could recognize his voice anywhere.

"Yes, sir."

"When I get those kids, I'm going to make them regret ever being born," Hayden mumbled. "Keep moving."

Several large shadows emerged around her and she held her breath as they moved past her hidden body and further into the woods. She could see four men, but she knew there must be more. Never before had it felt like she lived in a prison until that moment. She'd always tried to look at Jessup as a boarding school or orphanage – anything that made it seem more hospitable. Now, there was no ignoring the truth.

A few more agonizing minutes passed before she saw Ryker move. He stood, though he stayed crouched down as he made his way toward her. Without a word, he helped Maggie to her feet. He grabbed her face and turned it toward his.

"Move slowly and follow me," he mouthed silently.

She looked from him to the Remos searching in the distance. They were still so close. Ryker moved her face toward him again and raised his eyebrows. She nodded.

They moved slowly, deliberately. Maggie couldn't help but continue to glance at the Remos heading away from them. She was terrified that at any moment one of them would turn around. She also realized that more Remos could enter the woods at any time, and soon, her head was spinning in circles, anxiously scouring the area. It amazed her that Ryker was focused solely on what was in front of him. She could see his eyes scan the area ahead, but they did not move away from their target. His movements were fluid, natural and scary. He moved with the stealth of a well-trained Remo.

More time passed and the Remos finally moved out of sight, even their noises were lost to the woods. Still, neither of them spoke. As Maggie started to relax, she felt a pang of guilt. Where were Jules and Luke? How had she not thought of them before? Hours had gone by since she'd first entered the woods and run into Ryker. Hours.

"What happened to Jules and Luke?" Her voice came out cracked and strained, and she realized how thirsty she was.

"We split up." Ryker didn't look back but there was something in his tone.

"When? Why?"

"It was…it made the most sense."

She grabbed his arm, forcing him to stop and turn toward her. "Tell me what happened."

He took a deep breath and rubbed the back of his neck. "I told them I had to find you and that they should start moving. There was no point in all three of us waiting, so we agreed to meet up in town."

"In town?" None of them knew the area well. They only went to town under well-supervised outings.

"At the movie theater. It was the one place we all knew." Ryker half smiled, but there was fear in it. Maggie crossed her arms, waiting for him to explain. He sighed. "Luke's leg was pretty messed up. He could barely walk. I'm worried about how far he could go."

She shook her head. "But he could walk on his own, right? Did Jules say how she was going to get back into the center?"

Ryker scratched his chin as he looked out at the woods around them. "She promised to get him to the theater. Listen, in case we get separated and there are too many Remos for us to get there—"

"Why—"

"There are a lot of people after us, we don't have time to worry about Jules," he yelled suddenly. Her temper bubbled in her throat, but before she could speak, he sighed. "I'm sorry. We just need to have a back-up plan. I should've told Jules, but I just didn't think of it at the time."

The anger fell away as Maggie saw the anxiety in his eyes. "It's ok. She'll be fine."

He nodded. "If we do get separated, meet at the old cemetery. The one we always passed going in and out of town. You know which one I'm talking about?"

"Yes."

They continued in silence. Maggie's thoughts were consumed with their friends and the Remos after them. She feared what would happen if Hayden got a hold of them, and the guilt of forcing Jules into something she so adamantly didn't want to do was even worse. As the sun began to rise around them and their growling stomachs grew louder, neither spoke nor slowed. They were fueled by something else – fear. But more importantly, by the need to find their friends.

Chapter Seven

Progress felt slow. Maggie and Ryker continued through the woods, staying clear of the nearby road where the Remos would be patrolling, however, they both wanted to move faster. Finally, across an open field, buildings appeared on the horizon and signaled the town's location. They were nearly there. Ryker looked up and down the tree line, realizing there was no way to get to the town without going into the open.

"We can make a run for it," Maggie suggested.

"No, we should walk across. We'll be less likely to draw attention."

They looked at each other for a moment, both knowing the danger they were putting themselves in, and stepped into the field. Maggie steadied her breathing as they made their way into the city, but even when they were safely amongst the outer buildings, her heart rate didn't slow. It only beat faster. They were walking into the lion's den. After passing through several residential areas, they finally entered the city center that they knew held the theater.

"We need new clothes," Maggie said. They were standing in an alley preparing to enter the main streets.

Ryker looked at his clothes and then at hers. Not only were they identical center-blue, but they were also both covered in mud. "You're right."

They went onto the main street and walked past several doors before coming to a small clothing store. A shrill bell rang as they entered, sending Maggie's heart to her throat, but she was relieved to see the store was completely empty.

"Make sure to put on a few layers," Ryker whispered.

They both immediately began searching for clothes that would fit, and more importantly, help them blend in. She couldn't help but be amazed by the variety. Shirts and pants in all different colors and materials. She wished she had more time. Shaking her head, she made herself focus. Maggie grabbed a handful of items and went into the dressing room. As quickly as possible, she changed, putting on several layers as instructed.

When she stepped out, Ryker was waiting in a new outfit.

"How do I look?" He smiled.

She laughed. "Almost normal." She looked around, but still, no one was nearby. "How are we going to pay for all this?"

His smile grew. "They said that we're criminals.

Guess they were right."

Casually, they walked to the front of the store. Just as they reached the door, a short man appeared behind them.

"Sorry, I was in the back restocking. This tends to be our quiet time of day. Is there anything I can help you with?" The man was smiling and didn't appear the least bit suspicious.

"No, we were just looking, but thank you," Ryker said.

"It's a very nice shop," Maggie added.

She pushed Ryker out the door. The fear of being caught was making her nervous and she worried she would give them away. She hurried out after her brother and slammed directly into him. He was frozen solid, staring at two large Remos standing in front of them.

"Sorry," Maggie said, realizing she'd pushed her brother into one of them.

"You should be more careful," the Remo answered and turned away, but his partner stared at them both. She shifted uncomfortably under his narrow gaze.

"Why are you two not in school?" the Remo finally asked.

"School?" She was surprised by the question. She was certain the man had recognized them.

"It's Thursday morning, and you should both be in school. Why is it that you are not?"

"We're both sick," Ryker said. Even Maggie looked

at him, not believing he would use such a poor excuse.

"So, while feeling so sick you couldn't make it to school, you decided to go shopping?"

"We came out for medicine, but I saw the store and begged him to let me go in. We were only in there for a second. We didn't even buy anything. I just wanted to take a look." Maggie could feel herself babbling.

"Show me your ID." The Remo held out his hand.

She knew what he wanted but didn't move. Every child in the country had a digital chip inserted under the skin on his or her left arm, just below the elbow. This ID held all the information about them – name, age, where they lived, family history, blood type, and more. It was how the government kept track of the population.

When neither of them moved, the Remo grabbed Ryker's arm and jerked it forward. He yanked the sleeve up and scanned the ID that was suddenly visible. The portable machine beeped, indicating the scan read, and his arm was released. The Remo stared at the screen, waiting for the ID to come up. Maggie glanced nervously at Ryker. He gave a small, barely noticeable, nod. She knew immediately what he was going to do, and yet he moved so quickly, she was momentarily frozen in awe.

He ran, but without hesitation, the Remos were right behind him.

"You know where to meet me!" He shouted as he made it across the street and around the corner.

His words jolted her from her place, but they also

caught the attention of the second Remo. He stopped running and shouted, "I'm going for the other one!"

Maggie didn't wait for him to finish his sentence. She turned and ran down the street, cutting into the nearest alley. Her heart raced as she weaved through the tight side street. She popped out on another main road, crossed it, and reentered the depths of the alley system on the other side. She couldn't tell how close the Remo was behind her, she could only hear her own breathing and footsteps against the pavement. Finally, when her chest hurt and her legs burned, she stopped. She was in a dark alley surrounded on all sides by tall buildings. The dank space smelled of rotting garbage emanating from nearby bins. Still, it was silent. She'd lost her pursuer.

Maggie exhaled. She had no idea where she was in relation to the theater, but she was relieved to be momentarily safe and prayed Ryker was too. She walked to the end of the alley and peered out. Two Remos, different from those she'd just escaped, stood further down the street. She knew a child alone at that time of day would arouse suspicion, especially if they were searching for runaways, but looking around the alley, she saw no other choice. There was a fire escape to the roof which was too high to reach, and the few doors that were there were locked. She took a deep breath and stepped out into the bright sunlight.

She forced herself to walk casually, though she worried this was impossible. Every muscle in her body was tense. Despite the cold breeze, sweat rolled down her back. She wouldn't allow herself to look at the Remos, knowing that would be even more suspicious. *Think like Ryker,* she told herself.

A few adults passed by on the street, paying her no attention, and this helped to calm her. But as minutes passed and there was still no sign of the theater, Maggie started to become frantic. She moved faster, her legs unconsciously propelling her forward. She wanted to ask someone for directions, but she knew better. Finally, she turned a corner and saw the theater a few blocks ahead.

Maggie glanced around cautiously but could no longer see any Remos. She picked up her pace, but with only two blocks to go, she was pulled into an alley. She fought to pull free of her attacker's grip and they both fell hard to the ground. She scrambled to her feet, turning toward her attacker with fists in the air. It was Jules.

For a moment, Maggie was frozen in disbelief, but when her friend smiled, she threw her arms around her, hugging her tightly. It wasn't until she had Jules in front of her that she realized how heavy her absence had been weighing. And for a moment, everything was all right.

"Are you ok?" she asked.

"I'm fine, tired." Jules looked to Maggie's clothes. "Nice outfit."

"I have a few layers on." She started pulling the outer

most off. "Here, change."

"It's all right."

"You're a re-ed kid a mile away. Change." Maggie held out a long sleeve shirt.

Jules nodded. In just a few seconds, she looked like a completely different person. It amazed Maggie what a difference it was to see her in non-center clothes.

"Where's Ryker?"

"So, you haven't seen him?" She explained how they were separated, then it dawned on her that they were still missing one other person. "Where's Luke?"

Jules' jaw tightened and she looked to the ground. "He didn't make it."

"What happened?"

"I tried to help him out of the woods, but his leg was so messed up. I think it was broken. Each step was excruciating for him, he couldn't put any weight on it and we were moving so slowly. The Remos were closing in right behind us. Luke told me to leave him, but I couldn't. He pushed me away, but when he tried to walk on his own, he fell to the ground. He was screaming at me to leave him, but I pulled him back to his feet. That's when he was shot."

Jules rubbed her face and began pacing.

"Was it a bullet?" Maggie remembered being shot at herself, and she feared the danger she had narrowly missed.

"A dart. Almost instantly, he had some crazy reaction.

It was like a seizure, but instead of shaking, he started to scream. The noise was so loud and every Remo was coming right toward us. I had no choice but to run. I swear...there was nothing I could've done."

"I'm so sorry I got you involved in all of this. I know you didn't want to come along."

She merely nodded and Maggie could see regret in her eyes.

"Why aren't you at the theater?" she asked, forcing her friend to focus.

"There are Remos all around it. I'm afraid...I wonder if Luke told them that's where we're meeting."

It suddenly made sense to Maggie why none of the other Remos had stopped her.

They were waiting for her to meet up with the others so they could take them all at once. Panic immediately grabbed hold of her as she realized Ryker was walking into a trap. They had no way of knowing from which direction he would come, and it was possible he was already there.

"I figured if I waited here I might run into you. This alley has the best sightline to the theater without Remos being too close by. I figured if they were prowling the other streets, you'd be more likely to come down this one," Jules said.

They both looked at each other, coming to the same thought at the same time. That was the road the Remos had wanted them to take. They had been funneled down it, and the only question that remained was had they gone too far? Were they already caught in the trap?

Chapter Eight

"We need to get out of here." Maggie glanced around the corner to the main street and could see no indication of any Remos.

"What about Ryker? He could be at the theater waiting for us." Jules' hands twisted in front of her.

"We have a back-up plan. He'll see all the Remos around here, like you did, and he'll go to the cemetery. The one we always pass leaving town. He'll know better than to get this close." She prayed it was true. Her stomach turned at the thought of Ryker already waiting for them at the theater, unaware they'd all be arrested the moment they got close.

"Maggie—"

"He's smarter than that." She said it more to reassure herself than her friend, then took a deep breath. "If we're already too close to the theater, they might arrest us if we try to backtrack."

"What choice do we have?"

Maggie walked passed Jules, heading to the back of the alley. It was a dead-end, but as she turned back, she noticed a small opening in the left corner. There was a narrow gap that ran parallel to the street between the building next to them and the one behind it. It was nothing more than a drainage area, but she was certain they would be able to squeeze through.

"Come on."

She slipped through the opening before Jules could protest. With her back pressed hard against one side, the other still rubbed tight against her chest. Maggie tried to keep her breathing shallow, but as she got further into the small space, the urge to panic rose in her throat. She swallowed hard, forcing her heart rate to stay calm. It was too dark to see where they would come out, but she could see the opening ahead. She picked up her pace, careful not to trip on the garbage and debris lying in her path.

"This was a bad idea," Jules mumbled as she struggled to keep up.

"Be quiet." Maggie stood just inside the drainage space, looking for any sign that Remos were waiting on the other side. It didn't lead to an alley but directly to a main road. An older couple was walking across the street, and further down, she could see someone opening a store. Nothing seemed out of the ordinary, but she knew that didn't mean Remos weren't hidden nearby.

"Can you see any Remos?"

"No, but they have to be here. We're only two blocks from the theater." She feared simply stepping out from their cover. They'd have nowhere to run, not with their path of retreat leading back into the trap.

"We might as well—"

"Wait a second."

A large group of children were walking down the sidewalk toward them. The kids were laughing and joking, while two adults urged them to hurry along. Maggie realized immediately it was a school trip. That's what they always looked like when they were taken out of the center, but these weren't re-ed kids. They had normal clothes.

"A group of kids is about to walk by. We have to jump out right after they pass and join them," she said. The kids looked to be a couple years younger than them, but she was confident they could pass as part of the group. They only had to make it away from the theater.

"You're kidding. There's no way that'll work."

"We don't have time to argue. Get ready." She knew it was a risk, but they had few other choices.

Maggie held perfectly still as the group passed. Not surprisingly, they were all so distracted by their own conversations, they didn't notice her standing in the shadows. Every muscle felt tense as she waited for the last of the group to walk by. She waited until they were just two feet passed her and stepped out. It was difficult to do so casually, but none of the kids looked back. She grabbed Jules' wrist and dragged her out.

"Come on." Maggie tried to smile as she pulled her closer to the group. She wanted any Remos that could be watching to assume they were just lagging behind the other kids. "Smile," she mumbled.

Jules rolled her eyes but forced a smile. They walked awkwardly behind the group, trying to look calm but finding it difficult to do so. Despite the chilly breeze, sweat dripped down Maggie's back, and though she tried not to look for Remos, she found it impossible to stop her eyes from darting around. They made it down the street and stayed with the class as they headed away from the theater. Finally, the students were led into a stone building that was a museum of some sort. She and Jules simply continued passed the entrance, and though the teachers looked at them curiously, neither tried to stop them.

They only knew the general direction to the cemetery, so they both looked for any familiar markers. This was made more difficult as they tried to follow alleys and backyards, any way to avoid the main streets. When the church finally came into view, they both stopped, but neither felt relief.

"They could be waiting for us," Maggie said.

Jules shook her head. "They would never guess we'd come here."

She seemed confident, but Maggie knew she was just

being comforting. She merely nodded and continued walking. They followed an old, worn stone path to the graveyard behind the church. When they arrived, Maggie could feel her concern for Ryker growing. What if he never showed up?

"I'm getting a little nervous just waiting here," Jules said. They had been in the graveyard, crouched low behind a tall tombstone, for over an hour. There had been no sign of Ryker.

"I'm not leaving here without him." She glanced at her friend but then looked away. She could see her anxiety, which only made Maggie feel even guiltier. It was her fault that Jules was there, but despite knowing that, she couldn't stand the idea of leaving Ryker behind. She heard footsteps coming up the path and looked back at Jules.

Her eyes widened as she tried to sit up, but Maggie grabbed her arm.

"It could be Remos," she mouthed silently.

They both held perfectly still as the steps grew closer. Maggie's eyes darted around, trying to figure out the best possible escape route, but hundreds of tombstones lay as obstacles in their path. Her heart raced as she tried to keep from panicking. A shadow suddenly blocked the sun and she slowly looked up, afraid of who had found them.

"Ryker!" She jumped to her feet and threw her arms around him.

"Finally." Jules stood up and stretched her arms.

"There are Remos everywhere," he said. "I tried to stay near the theater for as long as I could, in case you didn't notice. It got too bad. I had to get out of there. Where's Luke?"

They all crouched back down behind the tombstones as Maggie explained everything that had happened. When she finished, they sat in silence. The weight of their situation and the loss of Luke hung heavy between them.

"It was his decision to come," Ryker said finally.

"But I'm the one that left him behind," Jules said.

"Either of us would've done the same thing," Maggie said. Ryker tilted his head to the side and she narrowed her eyes at him. She could see he wanted to disagree.

"We need to focus on what we're going to do," Ryker said, looking away from her. "We need to get out of this city. We're just on the outskirts of Lansing, so I say we head further in. It'll be easier to hide in a bigger place."

They all nodded.

"And from this point forward, we stay together. No matter what," Maggie said.

He nodded. "No matter what."

As they stood and began making their way toward the city, Maggie tried to take account of the positive things. She had her brother and best friend, no longer was Ryker going to be transformed into a Remo, and now they were free to make their own decisions. Yet despite that, Luke crept to mind. Guilt circled along with him. She had started the plan for escape, and because of that, whatever misery he was now suffering was directly her fault. She swallowed hard but the guilt didn't go away. Maggie sighed, realizing she hadn't really expected it to.

Chapter Nine

They found the state capital building, however, they were only able to see it from a distance. As they got closer, more and more Remos appeared on the street and it got too dangerous to stay on the main roads. Moving through Lansing's alleyways was much worse than outside the city. The smell of decaying garbage was nauseating, yet did nothing to keep away their hunger. None of them had eaten for nearly 24-hours, and stomach growling had turned to painful stabs of hunger.

"I need something to eat," Maggie said finally.

"Same here." Jules leaned against a wall as her hands held her stomach.

"We need to get some money." Ryker glanced into a nearby garbage can but immediately looked away. "That's the only way we're going to get what we need."

"I'm sure we're perfect candidates for new hires," Maggie said. "I'll just go—"

She stopped as she saw movement in the shadows. A tall man moved toward them, and instantly, every muscle tensed.

"No one's going to hire a sorry bunch like you." The man's voice was scratchy, and as he got closer, Maggie could see how worn his clothes were. She relaxed slightly and the man laughed. "Thought I was one of them, didn't you?"

She glanced at Jules and back. "No."

He laughed harder. "So, where're you headed?"

"That's none of your business." Ryker stepped closer, placing himself between the girls and the stranger.

"I want to help." The man pushed his sleeve up, revealing clean skin. He had no ID and there was no sign one had ever been there. "I know a thing or two about outsmarting Remos and the like."

"Where's your ID?"

"I'm clean. Managed to avoid them all these years. I live underground and am happy to do so if it means I'm not cataloged." The man leaned against the wall and stretched his arms out wide in front of him. "You should know, there are always ways to make a buck around here, especially off the books."

"Yeah, how?" Ryker didn't trust him. Maggie could hear it in his voice.

"Me? I help reunite families, for a nominal fee, of course."

"How?" Maggie unconsciously stepped forward.

The man grinned. "It's easy. If any of your relatives are cataloged or have been arrested, their DNA is in the system. With a small prick of your blood, I can tell you who your parents are and where they are. Can even tell you about brothers, sisters, aunts, and uncles. Anyone you're looking for."

"The system just lets you look through it?"

"Well, you need to know a talented hacker. Luckily, I do."

"And how much does something like that cost?" she asked.

"More cash than you have." He looked at each of them, glancing from their faces to their covered arms. He tried to hide his grin but it held firm in his eyes. "Though I have been known to take payment in other methods. IDs, for example."

She glanced at Ryker. "Why would you want them?"

"That's another side business of mine, helping people become on the books, off the books. In order to do that, I need IDs." The man picked at his teeth, making Maggie's lip curl. "So, are you interested?"

"Yes," Jules said. Both Maggie and Ryker looked at her in surprise. "You guys want to convince me the DRM is terrible? Then tell me about my parents and what kind of people they are. Besides, I want to get this ID out of me. The only thing it's good for now is to help them track me down."

Maggie had to agree. She desperately wanted to

know who her parents were. After reading through their personal files, she knew they held no useful information. This was a real opportunity, and it might even convince Jules of the truth.

Ryker grabbed both girls' arms and pulled them away from the man. "Give us a second."

"Ryker—"

"I think you're right," he interrupted. "It's better not to have our IDs, and we might as well get something useful for it. Maggie, what do you think?"

She nodded. "Let's ask if he'll throw in some food."

Jules laughed and merely nodded as he turned back toward the man.

"Throw in something to eat, and you got a deal."

The man smiled and clapped his hands together. "Great. Follow me."

He led them further down the alley and around the corner. As they weaved through the city, the buildings around them became older and more decayed. The people were also less well dressed, dirty even, and in their new clothes, they stood out considerably. People stared as they walked. The man led them to a large apartment building that had smashed out windows and peeling paint. Maggie glanced at Jules, who shrugged uncertainly.

"What's your name?" Maggie asked as they climbed stair after stair to the fifth floor. The inside of the building looked as bad as the outside, and they had to be careful not to step on the abandoned furniture and trash that lay in their path.

"You can call me Simon." The amusement in his voice told her it wasn't his real name.

He led them down the fifth floor hall to a burnt orange door. It was covered in scratches and dents as if it'd been knocked in several times.

"What is this all about?" Another man appeared from a back room as they walked in.

"Be nice, Lewis, these are customers. The deal is, you do a blood run on each of them and we get their IDs."

"Don't forget the food," Ryker said.

Simon laughed. "Right. They also get something to eat."

Lewis grinned eagerly and waved them toward a computer sitting in the corner of the room. There were three screens set up and all looked very expensive, especially in contrast to the rest of the rundown apartment.

"All right, first we'll take your IDs, then we'll run the test. Agreed?" Lewis said.

They all nodded. Maggie presented her arm first, looking for the hundredth time at the chip imbedded in her skin. Simon pulled out a small machine that looked identical to a regular scanner.

"This will be a little…unpleasant," he said.

She nodded for him to continue. He placed the end of the machine on her arm, resting it against the ID, and holding it with both hands, he clicked a large blue button on the side. She could hear it rev up and engage. For a moment, she felt nothing. Then the machine clicked loudly right as a sharp pain blasted into her arm.

Maggie bit down, trying to keep her face calm, but heat radiated down her arm as the pain intensified. Finally, the machine let go. A four-inch-long incision ran down her forearm and though she put pressure against it to stop the bleeding, she could see the ID had been fully removed. Aside from the cut, there was no trace of it left. Simon removed Ryker's and Jules' IDs and then stored them in a massive safe in the opposite corner of the room.

"All right, let's run some blood tests. Who's first?" Lewis asked.

Jules stepped forward and held out the arm that was still bleeding. Lewis used a dropper to collect a small amount of blood. He did not speak as he worked to input the drops of blood into a square machine connected to the computer. His fingers flew rapidly across the keyboard. The screens changed over and over, moving from system to system – it was impossible to keep up.

But then everything stopped and the computer beeped two short sounds.

"Done." Lewis reached away from them, grabbed the papers that had begun printing, and then handed them to Jules. "Here is all the information in the system on your parents."

Maggie leaned in to read over her shoulder. Her mother was dead, having been killed during a raid. Her father, on the other hand, was unaccounted for. He could still be alive.

"My dad was a professor and my mom was a nurse. According to this, my mom was arrested after she supplied an unlicensed couple with conception drugs. There's no record of what happened to my dad."

"Running is almost as bad an offense as having a kid without a permit." Simon scratched his neck. "Seen people, especially suppliers, put away for longer than those that actually done something wrong. Your dad must've not been there when she was arrested, either that or he's dead."

"Next." There wasn't a trace of sympathy in Lewis, and Maggie's eyes narrowed at his lack of sensitivity.

"Ryker, you go next." She was standing close to Jules, keeping a hand on her friend's shoulder for support. He nodded. "Jules, at least you know the truth."

"How does that help? I was totally happy not knowing about them, not caring about them, but how am I supposed to just forget this? I really believed everything they told us."

"We'll figure it out." The machine chimed again and Maggie's eyes widened with anticipation as Ryker took hold of his printouts. "What does it say?"

"More useful stuff, I'm sure," Lewis mumbled.

She ignored him and walked to Ryker to read along

with him.

"Mom is dead. It says she died in childbirth." He glanced awkwardly at her. "She was arrested just after you were born and died shortly after while in custody."

"What about dad?"

He moved the other paper forward. "It doesn't say anything about either one of us."

"What?" Simon asked.

"According to this, he doesn't have any children. He was arrested for assaulting a Remo and died in custody." Both of his arms fell to his side.

"They must not have entered the information correctly, or maybe they just don't know he's our dad," Maggie said, disappointed that neither of their parents were alive.

"That's not possible." Simon shook his head. "This system is categorized by DNA. It's impossible for there to be a mistake."

"What do you mean?"

"Even if the information was input incorrectly, the system automatically searches for matching DNA. It's programmed to. So it would have discovered that your DNA matches your father's and then it would have automatically matched it."

"Then why doesn't it?"

"Because someone manually altered it to not match. It's the only way it wouldn't do so on its own." Simon snatched the pages from Ryker's hand and read them.

He pointed at Maggie. "This is your sister?"

Ryker nodded.

"Lewis, run her DNA. Let's see what it says."

She stepped forward and held out her arm. Lewis jammed the dropper into her cut, unfazed by the pain it caused, and took a few drops of blood. He then fed it into the computer. Once again, his fingers flew across the keyboard, moving the screen from one step to the next until the first profile appeared.

"Here's your problem," Lewis said as the printer began moving. "Your father isn't the same person as his father."

"What?" Maggie leaned in closer to read directly off the screen.

"Both of you are listed on his arrest record, but he's only a genetic match for you. Whoever made the change in the system had a lot of juice to pull it off. This is unheard of." He moved his head from side to side, cracking his neck loudly.

"Pull up her mother," Simon said. The entire group was leaning uncomfortably close to the screen. They were all curious.

As he began working once again, Ryker and Maggie looked at each other. She could see the same pain in his eyes that she could feel lurking in her own. He wasn't her brother, at least not fully. It was possible they were half brother and sister, but even then, why would someone want to alter the records? According to the arrest report, her father was still alive. She felt guilty to be excited by that, knowing it meant being excited to have a different father than Ryker. She looked back to the computer, waiting for her mother to appear, but all three screens went black.

"They're trying to trace me." Lewis typed faster, something she was certain wasn't even possible. Sweat dripped down his forehead as he leaned closer to the main screen in front of him. "The DRM knows I'm in the system. It's your mother. Her file was flagged."

"Flagged?"

"Set to trigger a detection warning should anyone try to access it without authorization. I've never seen anything like this." His voice strained. Suddenly, his fingers froze. His face was pale and his eyes wide as he turned toward them. "They're coming."

Chapter Ten

Maggie ran to the window, which confirmed what she had already heard. The sirens were getting louder as DRM vehicles surrounded the building.

"Maggie!" Ryker yelled.

She darted to the computer and grabbed the printouts. She folded the papers as they ran to the stairwell and descended as fast as they could. Ryker suddenly stopped. Footsteps echoed below them. They were too late, the Remos were already moving up. Maggie pushed open the nearest door, which led to the third floor, and they ran in behind her.

"Find an unlocked door!" she yelled.

They ran from door to door, jerking the handles, desperately searching for an escape.

"Over here!" Jules yelled.

All three of them ran inside the apartment and Ryker slammed the door shut behind them before locking it in place. They were breathing heavily as fear shook through their bodies. Maggie turned around, searching for another way out. Her heart stopped when she laid eyes on an old woman staring at them.

"Please help us." Ryker and Jules held their breath behind her.

"Come with me." The old woman moved further into the dilapidated residence.

Without hesitation, they followed her, knowing they had no other choice. The woman led them to a small bedroom crammed with furniture and knickknacks.

"You must hide in here. When they swarm like this, if they are intent on finding someone, they will search door to door," she said. "I won't be able to stop them."

Maggie hurriedly pulled Jules into the closet as Ryker slid under the bed. They pushed themselves as far back into the space as they could and slid all the hanging clothes in front of them. She could see the fear in her friend's eyes, but she could think of no words of comfort to offer. To deny the danger would've been an unbelievable lie. Minutes passed and she heard nothing. She took a deep breath, trying to calm her racing heart. After a few more minutes, she smiled, relieved to have avoided the Remos, but then pounding echoed through the small apartment. Immediately, her heart began to race again.

"No, I haven't seen anyone." The old woman's voice could barely be heard as heavy footsteps entered the apartment. "I really must protest. This is an invasion of my privacy."

"If you'd like to enter a formal complaint, you can come with us." The Remos' voice was harsh and taunting.

"That won't be necessary."

The footsteps grew louder as they entered the bedroom. It was impossible to determine how many there were as they surged through the tiny space. The closet door whipped open, and Maggie froze. Petrified.

"I told you, no one is here. I wouldn't allow random strangers into my home," the old woman insisted.

A hand poked through the hanging clothes, directly between Maggie and Jules' heads. They both held their breath as the hand extended further until it touched the back wall. It moved slightly to the left and then to the right, missing both of the girls by inches. Then, as quickly as it had appeared, it was gone.

"The apartment's clear. We apologize, ma'am, for any inconvenience," the Remo said.

The footsteps left the room, yet none of them moved. Maggie waited, listening for Ryker, but there was only silence. She mouthed to Jules not to move, but as she stepped out of the closet, the old woman walked into the room.

"They're gone. It's safe to come out."

Ryker pulled himself out from underneath the bed, having to move several boxes out of the way to do so. *No wonder they didn't find him under there*, Maggie thought.

She turned toward the woman. "Thank you. We'll leave right away."

"No, they'll still be in the building. You should sit tight for a few hours, and then leave once things have quieted down. You look like you haven't eaten or slept in days, I'll make you kids some food." Without waiting for their response, she left the room and went to the kitchen.

Ryker followed her, moving with a determination that put Maggie on edge. "Why are you helping us?"

The kitchen sat directly at the end of a short hall, just opposite the bedroom. It was small, with only enough room for one person to efficiently work. An opening below the cabinets looked out on a modest living room where the three companions stood and watched her bustle through the tight space.

"If I had to guess, I'd say you're illegals. Am I right?" She didn't stop moving.

They glanced at one another, unsure how to answer.

"My daughter was arrested for having an illegal child. You can imagine my feelings toward the DRM."

"We're not illegals in the way you might be thinking," Maggie said. Ryker shot her a stunned look, but she ignored it. "We recently escaped from a re-ed center."

The woman turned toward them. "The one in Jessup?"

She nodded.

"Did you know a boy by the name of Tristan?" The

hope in her voice was crushing.

"No, I'm sorry. It doesn't sound familiar," Maggie said.

"He would be much older than you children." She looked back to the work in front of her, finishing in uncomfortable silence. When she turned back to them, she handed each a plate of food. "Come sit in the living room."

The room was small and sparsely furnished. A light pink sofa with torn fabric and stuffing poking through sat in front of a worn coffee table. A small television was nestled in the corner and looked to be older than any of the woman's guests. Maggie sat on the floor, trying to force herself to eat slowly and savor the food, but it was difficult. She was starving. Neither Ryker nor Jules spoke as they both ate as fast as they could. The woman smiled.

"I thought you looked hungry. My name is Roxanne." She raised her eyebrows, waiting for their introductions.

Maggie glanced at the others, unsure if they should give such valuable information away, but Roxanne had already helped so much. She introduced each of them.

"Where are you headed?" she asked.

"We were going to try and find our parents, but that doesn't seem like it's going to happen now."

"Because they're all either dead or in jail." Ryker had a distant look in his eyes. Maggie knew he was thinking about the same thing she was.

"And they're not the people we thought they were." She was surprised by the bitterness in her voice.

Ryker grabbed her forearm tightly. It happened so unexpectedly, her heart jumped to her throat. He stared intensely at her until she finally met his gaze. "Regardless of what that paper says, you are my sister. You know that, right?"

She didn't answer. She didn't know what to say. It amazed her how so few words could put such warmth in her heart.

"Maggie, this doesn't change anything. Our deal still stands. We stick together, no matter what." Despite his forceful tone, his eyes pleaded with her to respond.

She nodded. "No matter what."

+ + +

They ate in silence. Maggie could see Roxanne was eager to know more, but she patiently waited for them to speak. She understood what they were going through, even if she didn't know the details.

"The most pressing issue is why was your mother's file flagged." Ryker said suddenly.

"What do you mean, flagged?" Roxanne asked.

"That's why the Remos came, we were trying to find out who my mother was," Maggie explained. "I wonder if that means she's still free. Like they flag the files of anyone wanted by the DRM. Maybe there's a chance we could find her."

"This is a waste of time. Your mom is probably dead and they just don't know it. We should focus on getting out of the country, head for the border and start over," Jules said.

"I have to find her."

"Even if we find out her name or why she's flagged, what good will it do?" Jules pushed her plate with a hard shove, causing it to wobble noisily against the wood floor.

"If she is free, she'll be able to help us avoid being captured. We might even be able to have a family."

"You think your mother is still free?" Roxanne asked, trying to keep up.

"It's possible," Ryker said.

"You should know – this is an election year, one of the biggest we've had in decades. The Traditionalists have a candidate that has openly announced if he wins, he'll repeal the Reproduction Act of 2055. The Evolutionaries want nothing but to keep everything status quo, and right now, they have the upper hand. They passed a law saying anyone found guilty of breaking the Reproduction Act can be convicted as a felon, thus eliminating their right to vote. Traditionalists are scrambling to get this struck down by the Supreme Court, but it's a long process," Roxanne said.

"Everyone knows this is an election year. What does that have to do with us?" Jules crossed her arms.

"If the Traditionalists win the election, our parents will be released from prison," Maggie said, thinking aloud. It seemed so farfetched.

"It's possible." Ryker nodded, though his gaze was far away.

"Oh my God," Jules said. "We just need to stay in-country, free, long enough for the election to be over."

"Exactly." She was suddenly consumed with the idea of her new family.

"It's a long shot, but it's possible," Roxanne said. "The Evolutionary candidate has a long history with the party and is extremely popular. Her father was Vice President when the Reproduction Act was first passed. She's climbed up as a Senator fast, is the current Vice President, and is now trying to make the final ascent. It's amazing, but between her and her father, there's been a Fullbrook in office since the act's inception. It'll be an uphill battle for the Traditionalists."

"So, where do we start?" Jules' depression disappeared in an instant, replaced with determination.

"We need to find out my mother's real name. Since we have no idea where she's from, and her file is flagged, I can only see one way we'll be able to do that. We need to talk to my dad." Excitement grew in Maggie's chest as she said the word dad aloud for the first time.

"It will be impossible to get into the prison to see him. We'll be arrested instantly." Ryker's voice was flat and dismissive.

"Anyone entering a prison to visit an inmate must have a scannable ID, unless you're over the age limit," Roxanne said. As a provision within the act, anyone over the age of 55 was not required to get an ID. Their DNA was still categorized within the system, but that was seen as less invasive.

"My point exactly." Ryker cracked his knuckles one by one.

"But you can call without an ID. It must be scheduled in advance, and they have the right to listen in."

"How long does it take to schedule?" Maggie asked.

"24 hours' notice. They will want a phone number where they can reach you. The prison calls you, not the other way around."

"If they know that it's us calling, they'll trace it," Jules said.

"That's why this isn't a good idea." Ryker stood and began pacing.

"I know a phone you can use," Roxanne said. "My nephew works with computers and he can provide an untraceable number. I can take you there once it gets dark. Unfortunately, with the raid, that's probably the safest option."

Maggie and Ryker looked at one another, both nervous to follow a woman they barely knew through the city at night.

"Let's do it." Jules spoke before either of them could say otherwise. Maggie merely nodded, knowing it was a risk they were going to have to take. It might lead them to her mother, and in a few months, the rest of their families. They had to try.

As darkness settled in, they finally left the apartment. Roxanne warned that Remos often patrolled the area and they would all have to be extremely careful. The streets seemed much worse in the darkness of night. The buildings looked even more dilapidated, almost falling apart from the inside out, and the few people on the streets wore dark clothes, along with hoods and scarves to mask their faces. Everyone was on edge.

After a few blocks, they arrived at a rundown house that Roxanne insisted was their destination. Jules glanced uneasily at Maggie. They entered the structure and it appeared deserted, though Roxanne moved with a familiarity that offered a small level of comfort. The main hallway curved through the house, passed a caved-in staircase and kitchen with no ceiling, to a narrow staircase that descended below the house. Every step creaked under the weight of the trespassers, silenced only once they reached the cemented bottom. They traveled through three doors and took several turns before stopping in front of a large, metal wall. Roxanne slid it to the right along the hidden rails to reveal a bright room.

It was large and looked like it had previously consisted of two separate rooms. The floor was covered in a dark red carpet, and different colored chairs and sofas sat in a semicircle with a square table in the middle. Against the far wall stood a desk with a small laptop on it, which was snuggled next to yet another sofa – this one olive green.

"It's safer if the rest of the house looks deserted," Roxanne said as she took off her scarf. "Remos think this entire place is abandoned."

"Did you have any trouble?" A young man walked toward them.

As he got closer, Maggie's breath caught in her throat. He looked to be Ryker's age but slightly shorter. His eyes were vivid green, almost emerald, and they sparkled even in the basement room.

"No." Roxanne gave him a hug and then turned toward the others. "This is Wick."

"I'm Maggie, this is Jules, and my brother, Ryker," she introduced.

Wick gave a half smile and nod of acknowledgement. "So, what can I help you with?"

Maggie explained what they wanted to do, and how Roxanne said he could help. Wick laughed. "I can take care of that no problem." He walked to the computer and began typing. "What's his name?"

Maggie pulled the folded paper from her pocket. She felt slightly embarrassed that she couldn't remember her own father's name. "Henry Kerns."

Wick continued typing. "I've set the appointment up for tomorrow. The phone number I provided is untraceable, so don't worry. You should all stay the night here. It's too dangerous to be out this late. You really shouldn't have come now to begin with."

"Unfortunately, we didn't have much of a choice." Roxanne walked to one of the sofas.

"Are you sure they won't be able to track us?" Ryker asked.

Wick smiled, amused. It was hard for Maggie not to stare. "Yeah."

"I'm asking for a reason. The last person who said that was tracked, and we were nearly arrested." Ryker's face was stone.

"It'll be all right. Don't worry." Wick lay down on the sofa next to the computer. "Try and get some sleep."

Maggie took one of smaller sofas, then Ryker and Jules followed suit. She closed her eyes, and despite all that had happened, she could feel exhaustion taking over. She was out in seconds, dreaming of the future that might still be.

Chapter Eleven

The morning arrived earlier than Maggie would have liked. Roxanne and Wick were already up and talking near the exit. She couldn't hear what they were saying, but it was obvious that Roxanne was leaving. She had her scarf wrapped securely around her head and coat buttoned up tight. Wick gave her a quick hug and then she was gone.

Maggie was sad to see her leave. Though they had only known each other for a short time, the woman had shown them more kindness in the last twelve hours than any other adult had. She thought of Ms. Larson and sighed.

"Are you hungry?" Wick glanced at her as he walked back to his computer.

She sat up and saw the others were still asleep. "No." Her stomach growled loudly, betraying her words.

Laughing, he leaned to the left of his computer, fished out a small bag from an open cabinet, and tossed it to her. Maggie smiled as she examined the plastic wrapping. It was a muffin.

"They're not great, but they won't kill you."

As she unwrapped it, she moved to the sofa nearest him. "How long have you lived here?"

"Not long. I only stay here occasionally. I find it's best to move around as often as possible." He typed as he spoke, needing little concentration as his fingers moved.

"Where's your accent from?" It sounded like an odd blend of English and American, but she couldn't quite place it.

He laughed.

"I didn't mean—"

"This is what we all sound like, kids that grew up illegally. You're actually the surprising one. It's not often someone that sounds so mainstream would be coming around a place like this."

Maggie picked at the muffin, eating little bits at a time. "We've only been out of the center for a couple days."

Wick looked at her. "Which one?"

"Jessup."

He nodded and looked back to his computer. "They nearly sent me there once. About three years ago, some Remos picked me up and threw me in a car to drive me out. One of the doors didn't lock properly, so I was able to jump out. I ran into the woods and they couldn't find me." He stopped typing and looked at her. "Is it as bad as they say? At Jessup, I mean."

She looked up from her muffin. There was a curiosity in his eyes but also sympathy. "No, most of the kids like it. If you can't remember anything of life before the centers, it's really not a bad place, but once you know what was taken from you, it's hard to see it the same way again."

"Remos work there?"

She nodded. "They're not that bad."

He laughed softly. "If only that was true."

Maggie looked back at her muffin, suddenly feeling self-conscious.

He cleared his throat uncomfortably. "Do you want me to fix your ID? I can update the information so if a Remo scans it, you'll come up as an upstanding citizen." He smiled.

"Thanks, but I've already taken care of it." She rolled up her sleeve to show him the long incision. His forehead crinkled as he bit his lip. His eyes went from the cut to hers and back. "What is it?"

"Who did that?"

"The guys that ran our blood through the system. We didn't have any cash, so they took them." It suddenly dawned on her that they had no way to pay Wick for his help. "But we can figure out some way to pay you."

He shook his head. "You don't have to pay me. Why did you give them that? Do you know how valuable it is?"

"What do you mean?"

He took a deep breath. "A young person without an ID can only be one thing – illegal. For adults above a certain age, it's not required, but for us it is. If a Remo stops you and sees that, he'll know you're on the run."

"But if I kept it, he'd know the same thing."

"Not if it was reprogrammed. You can get that done on the street, then when it's scanned, it will say you're not a criminal."

"So what do we do?" Maggie pulled her sleeve down, covering the evidence of her naivety.

"There's nothing you can do. I don't know anyone that has spare IDs. They sell fast. You'll have to be extra careful now. It'll take one look from a Remo, and you'll be arrested."

"Have you heard anything yet?" Ryker was awake. He walked over and sat next to Maggie on the sofa. His eyes flicked between the two of them and narrowed. "What's going on?"

"Nothing, we were just talking," Maggie said. Her stomach was once again tight with worry but she knew it would do little good to tell the others. It would only make them anxious, and since there was nothing that could be done about it, it was best not to say anything.

Jules woke up shortly after and she and Ryker each ate a stale muffin. Wick explained he'd found a stash at an old supermarket just before it was closed. None of them commented on the fact the food was stolen – everyone in that room was a criminal. The day wore on slowly and only the anticipation of the call kept them awake. It was late in the afternoon when a sharp ring interrupted the monotony.

"You'll be able to speak as if he's right here in the room. Everything is being routed through the computer," Wick explained as he began typing. "Ready?"

Maggie nodded.

"Hello? This is Henry Kerns. You requested a call? Who is this?" Her heart raced at the sound of his voice.

"How do I know it's you?" Maggie surprised even herself with her lack of trust.

The man laughed, though there was sadness to it. "I don't know how you want me to prove it."

"Fair enough." She took a deep breath. "My name is Maggie. I'm your daughter."

"I…I don't know a Maggie," Henry said.

She scrambled for her father's profile and scanned for her old name. "Charlotte."

"What? Charlotte?" His voice broke slightly. "I don't understand. How do you know who I am?"

"I escaped—"

Wick started typing madly. "It's fine. I have everything under control. Keep talking," he whispered.

"I escaped from the reeducation center and got a blood test. That's how I tracked you down, but my –"

"Reeducation center? No, that can't be right. That

wasn't part of the deal. She was adopted." Henry mumbled to himself and she could barely make out his words. She leaned closer as she strained to hear. "They agreed. She promised. Charlotte was adopted. This isn't right."

"Henry? I know this is a lot to take in, but my mother's file was flagged. I don't know why. I need to know her name so I can find her."

"If you really were at a center, then everything they said was a lie…. Oh my God. You need to stop asking these questions." Terror ruled Henry's voice.

Ryker and Jules stared intensely at the screen but said nothing. Maggie looked to Wick who was still typing frantically, but he nodded for her to continue.

"I need to know who she is. What's her name?"

"I can't tell you. You'll only make this worse. Please stop. Just get somewhere safe and stay hidden." His voice was desperate.

"I have a right to know!"

"It's because of who she is that I can't tell you."

"Have you ever heard of a boy named Ryker? Do you have any other children?" Ryker interjected. Maggie waited for her father to answer, silently praying the DNA had been wrong.

"No, I'm sorry. I don't know who that is. I only have one child, *had* one child. Charlotte, your mother loved you very much, you need to know that. She tried her best to keep you safe. She's—

" His voice cut off and was replaced by muffled grunts.

"Did you lose the connection?" she asked.

"No," Wick said, still typing.

The scream was so sudden that it sent Maggie's heart to her throat. Her hand unconsciously grabbed Wick's chair to steady herself. It was her father, screeching into the receiver. She could hear the panic in his voice, the agony.

"Charlotte! Run! Stay hidden!" Between his screams, Henry could barely form words. There were other inaudible voices in the background and she knew he wasn't alone. "I love you."

Then there was only silence. They all listened, waiting.

"It's still connected," Wick whispered. His fingers clicking on the keys offered the only reprieve from the heavy quiet.

"So predictable, the mind of a criminal." Maggie tensed as Hayden's unmistakable voice seeped through the line.

Chapter Twelve

"Hello, Ms. Ward. I assume your co-conspirators are there as well…most of them anyway. Are you curious about what happened to Mr. Williams? If you don't recall, that's the boy you abandoned in the forest with a broken leg."

Hayden's voice sent shivers down Maggie's spine, yet she couldn't stop listening. She looked at Ryker and Jules – both had wide eyes as they stared, mesmerized.

"He was sent to a high security center, where I believe he had his arm broken. According to the report, it was a student attack. Or perhaps it's extended punishment for his participation in this little excursion of yours. Any idea what's going to happen to your father, dear old Mr. Kerns? Imagine the trouble that awaits all these people because of you." He paused. "I very much look forward to speaking about this more in person."

Heavy footsteps thudded above them, finally breaking the trance that was Hayden's voice. Wick severed the connection as Jules ran to the door, pushed it open, and waved for the others to follow. But Wick shoved Maggie and Ryker out of the way, grabbing the olive green sofa and pulling it away from the wall. He ripped a large piece of dry wall loose and tossed it aside.

"Come on, get in!" He tore his laptop from the wall and waved at them.

"Is there a way to lock this?" Jules yelled as she tried to secure the door.

Ryker slid into the small space, followed by Maggie, though she stayed just at the mouth of the opening.

"Leave it!" Wick yelled

Jules was only two steps from the door when it burst open behind her.

"Hurry!"

The Remos moved too fast. Only feet away from Maggie's outstretched hand, a Remo clamped his hand around Jules' arm and yanked her backward off her feet. Maggie tried to get out of the tunnel, but Wick pushed her back as he crawled through the opening. Without hesitating, he pulled up the piece of dry wall and secured it back in place. Only then could she see the hefty metal locks as he shifted them into position.

"This won't hold forever. We have to move," he said.

She couldn't. She could hear Jules screaming for help as she fought against her attackers. Wick maneuvered by her, and without thinking, she lunged at the entrance. It was the only way to save Jules. He immediately grabbed her arms and pulled them off the locks.

"There's nothing we can do for her." He wrapped his arms tightly around hers and held her still. They could hear the room being destroyed. The locked entrance vibrated as Remos tried to break through. "If we don't move, they'll arrest us all."

"Maggie, we have to go," Ryker said.

Tears rolled down her cheeks as she nodded. Jules' screams grew quieter, and she knew her friend was being taken away. Wick released his grip, and as she crawled forward, he slipped behind her. Maggie noticed that he'd purposely placed his body between her and the door, but she didn't comment. They moved forward as fast as possible. No one spoke, and as more space was put between them and the Remos, the small area became eerily quiet. The tunnel was dark and poorly constructed, making some portions incredibly tight to get through. They spilled into a large cement room with several drains and pipes leading in different directions.

Wick pushed a small metal door over the end of the tunnel and entered a code into a miniature keypad. A low humming sounded as cement sealed around the hole – closing it off forever. Maggie's stomach tightened. There was no going back. Looking around, she could see they were in the sewer system, and the longer they stood there, the more the rancid smell invaded her senses.

"The sewer is only a rally point." Wick pointed to

another crude hole protruding into the cement. "Illegals have an entire network of tunnels throughout the city. They don't lead to everywhere, but they definitely help you get around."

Without speaking, they followed him into the next passage. It was just as poorly constructed. At the tightest point, they were forced to low-crawl on their stomachs to squeeze through, and Maggie had to swallow the sudden claustrophobia that threatened to bubble up. After turning so many times that she no longer knew what direction they were headed, they reached their destination. They climbed up a short vertical tunnel that led into a gymnasium.

"This is Franklin, one of the abandoned schools." Wick nodded for them to follow him. "Not sure if they teach you this, but when the act first went into effect, half the schools in the poor neighborhoods were shut down. It freed up money for the re-ed centers, and honestly, most illegals came from low-income areas. Suddenly, fewer kids needed public schooling."

The school was falling apart and it was obvious that it hadn't been used in years. Low-hanging wires crept from holes in the ceiling and lockers tipped on their sides laid as obstacles throughout the halls. Broken glass crunched under their feet with every step. Still, Maggie barely registered any of this. She felt like an empty shell. The guilt of leaving Jules was overwhelming. She was only feet from them. Why hadn't they helped her?

Wick pushed open a door on their left which led to a large open space. Maggie was amazed to see an entire community of people. All the interior walls had been knocked down, creating one massive room. Large tents were set up throughout and several fires burned in metal trash barrels, lighting the area and making shadows dance along the walls.

"What is this place?" Maggie was shocked by the number of people.

"I think I've been here before." Ryker stopped dead as he stared at the small world in front of them.

"This is Resistance headquarters for this area."

She grabbed Wick's arm, forcing him to stop. "Resistance against what?"

He laughed. "The DRM, of course. Did you really think people were just going to sit by while their friends and family were arrested?"

She felt foolish for asking, however, she'd never heard anything about a resistance before. According to her teachers, there were some that disagreed with the law, but they were rare and often criminals.

"How many resistance groups are there?"

"Loads. They're all across the country. Come on. There are some people you need to meet," Wick said.

Moving through the small walkways between the tents, they could see laundry hanging to dry and children playing board games. People living. Wick led them to a great red tent in the center of the space. Several adults, both men and women, stood around a stone fire pit in the middle of the tent, but as they entered, conversation immediately stopped.

"What's this?" one man asked. He was older and his face was worn.

"This is Ryker and Maggie. We were in the basement apartment when Remos stormed." Wick told them everything that had happened. Ryker jumped in to explain the DNA test and how they had come to meet Roxanne. However, Maggie was barely listening. She just wanted to be alone and have a moment to think.

"You said your name is Ryker?" a woman asked.

He nodded.

"I knew your mother. In fact, we all did."

"What?" He looked to Maggie, forcing her to listen.

"My name is Silvia. Your mother lived in the tent next to mine with you and your father. You were all with us for a few years here, up until you were taken."

"Taken?" Ryker shook his head.

"I'm sure you don't remember. You were so young." Silvia sighed. "A raid happened on the school. We have a warning system in place now to give us enough time to evacuate, but at the time, there was nothing."

"They arrested sixteen families, including yours." The man studied Ryker's face.

"According to the DNA analysis, my father didn't have any kids. He was arrested for assaulting a Remo." Ryker handed her the printouts.

"The DNA doesn't lie. He was your father, but he was taken alive. He never assaulted anyone." Silvia shook her head. "And your mother certainly didn't have a daughter, let alone die in childbirth when you were 17 months. You were four when the three of you were taken. These papers are all wrong."

The man's eyes narrowed and he grabbed the papers from her hands. He scanned them and then looked from Maggie to Ryker. "You're certain?"

"Of course, I am. She was my best friend." Silvia crossed her arms.

"I don't understand. Why would they say she died almost three years earlier then?" Ryker asked. "And why lie about who my father is?"

"They're hiding someone. A baby. But that doesn't make any sense." The man was speaking more to himself than the group.

"Why doesn't that make sense?" Maggie asked.

"Babies are always put up for auction. They'd be lost in the system with ease."

"Right. The auctions." She had momentarily forgotten about them. In order to lessen the burden on taxpayers, the baby auctions were started when the act was first initiated. Only people with valid birth permits that were unable to have children of their own were invited to the auctions, but only the rich ever won. Babies would go for hundreds of thousands of dollars. The younger they were, the better. Newborns had been known to bring in over a million.

"That's my point. Or maybe it's something else." The man stared at Maggie. "Who are you?"

She suddenly felt defensive as everyone's eyes shifted to focus on her.

"Leave her alone." Ryker stepped forward, squaring his shoulders to the man. "She just found this out along with us. That's why we tried to contact her father. We want answers."

The man shook his head. "No one is suggesting otherwise. But why would you think it was a good idea to contact her father? Wick, you should know better than that. Especially to do something so reckless from one of our safe houses. We don't have enough of them left for you to risk one on such ridiculous endeavors."

Wick looked to his feet. Maggie could see his teeth grinding together, although he said nothing.

"It wasn't ridiculous." She was sick of this – these people had no idea what they'd been through. "The DNA system wouldn't tell me who my mother was, so how else was I going to find out? Besides, I've never met my father before. How unreasonable is it to want to hear his voice?"

"What's your father's name?" the man asked.

"What's yours?"

The man smiled. "Jacob Tallon."

She shifted on her feet, feeling bad for snapping. "My father's name is Henry Kerns."

They all looked at one another but everyone shook their head. No one had heard of him.

"He's no one of note. That can only mean they're trying to hide your mother's identity." Jacob went to a computer sitting in the corner of the room. Within seconds, her father's file appeared on screen. "He has a brother in Connecticut, but he's also no one of importance."

Heat radiated in Maggie's chest each time he called them insignificant.

"We need to know who your mother is. If you would allow, I'd like to run your DNA again," Jacob said.

"That's not a good idea. Every time someone tries, the DRM sees. We'll lead them right here." She shook her head.

"We have the most advanced system in the city. It won't be a problem."

"We've heard that one before," Ryker said.

"It'll be all right," Wick said.

"You're the one who said that last time, and now we're one person short." Ryker's tone turned unsettlingly dark. "So, tell me, why should we believe you now?"

"Because if they can't find her mom, it can't be done."

Maggie took a deep breath and presented her arm. They had come so far to find information about her mother and lost Jules in the process. They couldn't stop now. Jacob moved quickly, taking a sample of her blood before Ryker could intervene. Immediately, he input it in the system. She held her breath as she waited to see if they would cause the ruin of the small community, but rather than screams and alarms, she heard the quiet chime.

"Oh my God." Jacob's body blocked the computer screen, then he slowly stepped out of the way, revealing her mother's picture at last. "Her mother is Elizabeth Fullbrook."

Rumblings of astonishment shot through the group as all eyes flickered between the picture on the screen and her.

Maggie laughed and shook her head. "You're telling me my mother is the Vice President of the United States? That's impossible."

"She's not just the Vice President," Silvia said. "She's the director of the DRM."

Chapter Thirteen

"That can't be the same person," Ryker said, pushing by the others to get a closer look at the screen.

"It is. She's the current Presidential candidate for the Evolutionists."

"I don't believe you." Maggie shook her head.

"She's on the news!" Someone shouted from the back of the group.

They all moved around to the other side of the fire pit, revealing a small TV with a flickering picture. The resemblance was uncanny, and Maggie moved closer to get a better look. The woman on the screen was the same from the photo, but seeing her stand at a podium, smiling and laughing, was too much. She couldn't believe it. She couldn't stop staring.

"I told you, laws don't apply to people with money," someone mumbled, followed by several murmurs of agreement.

"If that was the case, then she wouldn't have spent

her entire life in a re-ed center," Ryker snapped.

Jacob stepped forward, holding his hands up to quiet the others. "Don't you all see what this means? This is the ammunition we've been looking for. This will help us to stop the DRM once and for all. It's proof that those in power are using the laws for their own purposes."

All eyes shifted to Maggie with excitement. She looked back at them and could feel her heart rate increase. She desperately needed to be alone. Without saying anything, she ran from the tent and traced her steps back to the hallway from which they'd come. It was dark and cold, yet somehow provided more comfort than the warm tent she'd just left.

Her breathing was hard, though not from the run. Maggie leaned against the wall as she held her hands against her forehead. Her mind was spinning and she couldn't focus. Losing Luke, then Jules, her father's screams, and now her mother was one of them. She worked for the DRM, and not only that, she wanted to keep it around. How could her mother support a law that had kept them apart all that time? Tears welled and a lump began to grow in her throat.

"Why did you run away?" Ryker suddenly appeared in front of her.

Rage bubbled up inside of her and she could no longer contain it. "Why do you think? My mother is probably the reason my father is in jail. And because I insisted we track that woman down, my best friend is probably trapped in some horrible high security center!"

He walked closer and stood only a foot in front of her. "Maggie, it could be a lot worse. At least you know your dad is a good person and that he has a family. So it's not just the two of you…and you still have me."

She took a deep breath. "I know, you're right. Ryker, let's just go. Let's go to Connecticut and find Henry's brother. Maybe we can stay there until the election is over."

He didn't speak. She searched his face for an answer, but she could see something in his eyes, it was a fire she'd never seen before. He wanted to work with the Resistance. "Maggie—"

"I don't want to be someone's leverage!" It came out more forceful than she'd expected.

"Working with the Resistance is the best chance for a normal life." His tone hardened. "What do you think is going to happen to Jules? Huh? You think they'll just throw her back in Jessup and she'll be fine?"

"You're the one who said that once someone was taken there isn't anything we can do!" As soon as the words left her mouth, guilt flooded, calming her anger. She slunk to the floor.

He stood for a second before sitting next to her. "That was true until now. We have a chance to not only get Jules out, but all the kids in the center. We can stop this system from tearing apart more families."

She looked at the dirty floor trying to remember what life was like before she started questioning everything. Before she knew the truth. And for a flickering moment, she wished Ms. Larson had never told her anything.

"You know Roxanne isn't really my aunt." Wick moved further into the hallway, startling Maggie. Neither of them had known he was there, and she wondered for how long he'd been listening. "I'm not related to her at all. My parents were killed when I was nine, right in front of me. They didn't even try to arrest them." He shook his head. "I was able to get away, more luck than anything else. The Resistance helped to look after me, at least at first."

"Wick—"

He crouched down in front of her. "No one knows the desire to leave this place more than me, to leave this all behind. And you're right. You shouldn't let the Resistance use you as leverage. To trust them would be a mistake."

"Listen, just because you—"

"Ryker, isn't it?" Wick and Maggie turned toward him. Her brother's face was dark, but even in the dimly lit hall, she could see his anger.

"Yeah. And whose side are you—"

"You shouldn't speak about things you don't know." He turned back to her, though she was still looking at her brother. Rage burned in his eyes at Wick's condescending tone. "But if we do this together, Maggie, we can do it our way."

"And how do we know we can trust you?" Ryker asked.

"I didn't leave you behind before, did I?"

"Tell that to Jules."

"Ryker, stop," Maggie said. She looked down. Her hands were covered in dirt and grime. She knew, in her heart, that if she had let the DRM take Ryker, Jules and Luke would be all right. Her selfishness had caused this. She had to do whatever she could to make it right. She looked up at Wick, and despite the darkness, the emerald in his eyes still shined. "What do we need to do?"

He smiled. "We need proof that your father and mother were together. Even something as simple as a photograph – anything that will prompt people to demand that a public blood test be done. If we just show up at a news station, we'll be arrested. It wouldn't be the first claim like this. Once we have something, we'll send copies to all the major networks in the country and include the database print out. Someone will run it."

"But we don't have anything like that."

Ryker smiled, though there was no joy behind it. "Guess we do have to go to Connecticut."

Chapter Fourteen

Two days after their decision to leave, they still hadn't departed. They were gathering supplies but Maggie couldn't figure out why it was taking so long. Ryker spent his time being brought up to speed on Resistance activity over the last few years. He watched the uncensored Traditionalist candidate on the news whenever possible, something they'd never been allowed to do at Jessup, and he also watched every report on Maggie's mom. Although the Traditionalist candidate fascinated Maggie, she couldn't stand watching her mother and knew Jules couldn't wait.

When her frustration finally got the best of her, she followed the hallway from the small community and continued until she found a set of doors leading outside. They were sealed shut by a thick layer of cement that seemed to encase the doorway. She pulled at them, but they didn't budge. Irritated, she traced her way back to the gymnasium and the hole in the floor. As she looked down into the tunnel, she was surprised by the darkness. She hadn't remembered it that way. Taking a deep breath, she lowered herself down.

She wasn't sure which direction would lead to the surface, and the phone she had secretly borrowed from the Resistance offered little help in navigating the unmarked tunnels. She told herself that if she hadn't found it within an hour, she'd go back. But after only half an hour, she found a tunnel that went upward. With all her strength, she pulled herself to the top, using her legs as wedges along the way.

Carefully, she pushed open the cover and cold air rushed in. She was behind a rundown house with no one in sight, but still, she repositioned the cover before moving to the street. The dead of the street was unnerving. The neighborhood was nothing more than a shell of what had once been. She took out the phone and quickly located her destination on the map – the regional DRM office.

When she finally reached the building, she was surprised to see it didn't stand out from the neighboring offices. It could have housed any corporation. People were on the street, though they were obviously not afraid of the DRM – they were all legal. Several Remos stood just inside the entrance, scanning everyone that entered and left. She was certain this was where they'd taken Jules. They'd want to ask her questions about the escape and this was the nearest DRM location. Maggie followed the building around to the back, but thick walls with barbed wire along the top sealed all the alleyways.

"You have to be kidding me," she mumbled angrily.

She continued down the street until she finally found an open alley. Looking up, she could see the fire escape went to the roof, though she couldn't reach the bottom rung. Ignoring the rancid smell, she tried to push a dumpster closer, but it was too heavy. She exhaled in frustration as she climbed on top, and though it put her high enough, she was too far to the side to reach the rung.

Maggie took a deep breath and jumped. Her hands closed tightly around the bottom step, but as her weight jerked, the ladder clicked loose and slammed down. She fell hard on her back and rolled out of the way just in time to avoid being hit by the metal post. Maggie laughed nervously as she stood and began climbing. The wind hit her hard at the top, but she ignored the chill. She moved along the rooftop, stepping easily from building to building until, finally, she reached the edge of the DRM property – distinguishable only by thick barbed wire.

Looking down, she could see small buildings with grated windows set up within the alleyway. Her breath caught in her throat with excitement. Holding cells. Jules had to be there. Studying the barbed wire, she wasn't sure how to get through without being cut, but if that was necessary, she was prepared. She reached out to grab part of the wire when a hand snatched her wrist and pulled her away.

She turned and swung her free hand at her attacker, but he ducked out of the way.

"It's me!" Wick whispered.

Maggie pushed him back, forcing him to release his grip. "What are you doing?"

"I should ask you the same thing." His eyes darted around, only meeting hers every few seconds.

"Did you follow me?"

"You looked like you were going to do something stupid. We need to get out of here."

"Go ahead. I came here for a reason." She turned back to the barbed wire.

"Yeah, I know. You want to help your friend. I don't know what makes you think you can break in there and get her out, but that's suicide," he said.

She looked back at him. "Why do you care?"

"We have a plan, a good one, and you're about to mess it all up." His voice was harsh and direct.

"I'm sick of just waiting around—"

Wick lunged forward and covered her mouth, silencing her voice.

"Are you crazy? If they realize we're this close to the line, they'll have Remos out here in seconds." He stared firmly at her. "They have motion detectors all around the perimeter. We won't make it twenty feet past the line before they surround us."

She nodded reluctantly and he removed his hand. "If you want to do this master plan of yours, then we need to start. We need to get out of here and get to Connecticut."

He smiled. "Whatever you say, let's just get off this roof."

They retraced their steps in silence. Maggie didn't want to leave without Jules, not again, but hearing her plan out loud made it suddenly seem crazy. She had been acting on impulse. Her frustration and guilt had motivated her, but not wisely.

"It can be a bit overwhelming when you first experience the DRM like this," Wick said suddenly. They were walking along the city streets, nearing the residential area.

"Is that right? Until now, I never knew what Remos were like." It annoyed her that he thought she knew so little. She was certain she'd had more direct contact with Remos over the last few years than he ever had.

Wick laughed. "I'd be willing to bet your experiences were a lot different inside than they are here. Still, that's not what I meant. I was talking about meeting up with the Resistance. When people come here, they see a chance to make a change, to do something to right the wrongs done to them. Some can't help but throw themselves into it completely."

Maggie glanced at him and then to the pavement under her feet. "That must be what Ryker's trying to do.

But how do you right a wrong done to someone you may never see again?"

"You help someone else and hope that somewhere in the universe it balances out."

She looked at him again and found he was staring at her. Her face suddenly felt warm. "Do you believe that's possible?"

"For it to balance? I think people make decisions that determine if it's possible to ever regain balance. Too many wrongs, serious wrongs, and no, it never will. But a couple of wrongs? Yeah, that can be put right."

"Serious wrongs. Like abandoning someone? Killing someone? That kind of thing?"

"You didn't abandon anyone, and you certainly didn't kill anyone. Your friend made a mistake by going to that door. It's that simple. There wasn't enough time for her to get back." Wick turned down a driveway and led her to the backyard. It was a different place from where she'd been earlier.

"I could've tried."

"And then what would you have done when you were arrested as well?" They climbed over two fences covered in vines and overgrown bushes. "A serious wrong isn't running when someone is after you, it's forcing someone to run because you're after them."

She nodded and smiled. "So why is it that you're so untrusting of the Resistance?"

"Do you feel they're trustworthy?"

They stopped in front of an old building, and from the few remaining letters on the side, she could see it was the school. Her eyes remained fixed on the dilapidated structure. "No. I don't know why, but there is something about those people. Maybe this is just what happens when you grow up in a center."

"No, you just have good instincts. You can't trust any of these people. They would sell all of us out in a minute if it furthered the cause."

Maggie laughed. "Don't sugarcoat it."

"I've seen them do horrible things." He shook his head. "It doesn't matter. You'll feel better once we get going."

Maggie was afraid to trust him, yet somehow she knew she already did. He led her to the back of the school to a large brick wall. Pushing some bushes aside, he revealed a small, open space at the base of the structure. Wick crawled through first and Maggie followed, though she had to lie on her stomach and army-crawl in order to fit. He stood on the other side with a hand stretched out. She hesitated for a moment before putting her hand in his, and he pulled her to her feet. Even then, he did not release his grip. They walked hand-in-hand through the school, back to the hidden community. Without breaking stride, they entered the red tent where Ryker and the others stood talking.

"We're leaving tomorrow."

"We're still working out the best plan." Jacob didn't

look up from the papers spread across the table in front of him.

"We're going to take the SUV, and we're going to drive," Wick said simply.

Maggie looked from him to Ryker. Her brother didn't seem impressed with the plan and, even more, he seemed suspicious. His eyes narrowed as he looked at Wick and she caught him glance from Wick's face to their intertwined hands. Her face grew warmer as their eyes met and she pulled her hand away, crossing her arms in front of her. She could feel Wick look her way, but she pretended not to notice.

"They have checkpoints at every state border," Ryker said, his eyes moving to Wick's once again. "We won't even make it out of Michigan."

"They have an SUV with a secret compartment that even the DRM's infrared can't see through. It's how they smuggle illegals across state lines. The only person that needs to have a valid ID is the driver."

"In case you haven't noticed, none of us do."

"I've reprogrammed my ID, it'll pass inspection. The only adjustment that needs to be made is to add a registered relative that lives in Connecticut."

"Is that hard to do?" Maggie asked.

"No, it's just a matter of going into the system." He smiled at her and she nodded awkwardly.

"That's a great idea. That way, if they suspect anything, they'll know exactly where we're going," Ryker said sarcastically.

"Unfortunately, Wick is right," Jacob said. "Whenever you drive across a state line, they log your answers to their questions. The most important is where you are headed. If you say you're going to Ohio, and then a few hours later try to cross into Pennsylvania, they'll want to know why you lied. The only way to drive to Connecticut is for them to think Wick has a good reason for doing so. Even still, it's risky to have that information in the system."

"Do you have a better plan?" Maggie asked.

"We have a system in place to move people across the country undetected. We'll use that."

"The underground railroad?" Wick shook his head. "We'd be involving way too many people."

"You guys seriously call it the underground railroad?" Maggie raised an eyebrow. "Like the slaves?"

Jacob smiled. "Seemed fitting to us."

"That's beside the point. Do you realize how many people we'd be involving?" Wick's arms flew through the air as he spoke.

"We just won't tell them the details," Ryker said. "If you can keep a secret."

"It has nothing to do with secrets. Do you know how difficult it is to conceal runners? Let alone two of you? The more people we involve, the harder that becomes."

"The railroad was set up specifically for these types of situations. It's the best option and it'll get them to

Connecticut the fastest."

"If it's undoubtedly the best option, why didn't we leave two days ago?" Maggie asked.

Jacob shrugged noncommittally. "These things take time to organize"

"I'm going with them." Wick looked at Maggie, who nodded immediately.

"You can take them to meet Morrigan, but she'll take it from there."

"So, we leave tomorrow then?" she said. Jacob and the others glanced at one another before their leader finally nodded.

"Good." Despite Wick's smile, Maggie could see the worry in his eyes. This was the best plan, but that didn't make it a solid one. It was a real risk and not even he could hide his concern. But she wouldn't be the person to say anything. She needed to help Jules, to get her out. She needed this plan to work.

Chapter Fifteen

"Do you drive a lot?" Ryker asked as they headed out of the city. It had taken only a few minutes to pack their supplies and leave. The goodbyes were short. The awkwardness that had been hanging between the two boys only grew worse once in the car. Ryker and Maggie sat in the back while Wick drove. Not only was he the only one with driving experience, but the tinted back windows also offered cover from prying eyes.

Wick laughed softly. "A couple times before."

"That's comforting," Ryker mumbled.

They continued in uncomfortable silence and Maggie resigned herself to looking out the window. After being on the expressway for a couple of hours, Wick pulled off and took a small road east. No one spoke as they went deeper and deeper into the woods. The sun was coming over the horizon, finally relieving them of the early morning darkness, and Maggie felt growing anticipation at the journey ahead.

"Morrigan should be meeting us here," Wick said as the car came to a stop. They were just off a small road, and with the vehicle no longer in motion, they were surrounded by silence.

"Have you met her before?" Maggie unclicked her seatbelt and leaned forward to stretch her back.

"Only once. She's very...direct."

A sudden loud knock on the passenger door window startled the three companions. A woman stood just outside the glass, staring at them. She was in her mid-thirties with short jet-black hair and dark eyes. She had a menacing demeanor. Wick immediately unlocked the car and she got in.

"Morrigan." Wick gave a stiff nod.

"You're fifteen minutes late." She eyed them guardedly.

"Sorry."

"What's the plan?" Ryker asked.

"We go on foot from here and will cross the border at one of the less-patrolled sections. Our contact in Ohio will be waiting on the other side to take you to the next border." Morrigan checked her watch and clicked buttons on the side of it. "We need to get moving."

"Is going on foot really the best idea?" Wick asked. "There are sensors all along the border, and if they catch us, there's no plausible reason for being there. If we cross in a car, we can talk our way over."

"That's too risky. The checkpoints are heavily

guarded, especially since word spread of runners. From the sound of it, they're a much higher priority than the typical re-eds." She tilted her head as she looked at him, but he gave no indication of knowing anything. She shrugged. "We go on foot."

Morrigan got out of the car and Ryker followed suit. She walked towards the woods, but Wick ran after her and grabbed her arm.

"Wait, we should—"

She turned sharply toward him, hovering only a foot away. "Wick, right?"

"Yeah, I—"

"I was told you would bring the runners here, and that's where your journey ends. You can keep your opinion to yourself as, from this point forward, what happens no longer concerns you." Morrigan's voice was firm.

"I'm coming with you," he said.

"No, you're not." She turned to Ryker. "Grab the equipment from the car."

Ryker nodded and moved to the back of the car, pulling out the two black backpacks filled with supplies. He positioned one on his back and walked to Maggie, holding the second out for her. Wick snatched it from his hand before she could take hold.

"Yes, I am." He secured the bag to his back.

"Get it through your head, we don't need you," Ryker spat. "This has nothing to do with you."

"Coming from the person who, until a few days ago, didn't even know there was a Resistance. You're in over your head and you have no idea the history at play here." Intensity blazed in Wick's eyes.

"He's coming with us." Maggie stepped forward.

Ryker stared at her. His face was tight with anger. "You're kidding me."

"It's your supplies," Morrigan said, looking at her watch once again. "We don't have time to sit here and discuss it. If you want him so badly, he can come, but we're doing this my way. That's non-negotiable."

Wick glanced at Maggie. "Understood."

Without hesitation, Morrigan moved into the woods. The pace was fast and no one spoke as they struggled to keep up. Everyone but Ryker. He was the only one unfazed as he moved through the forest with an eerie silence. After almost an hour, Morrigan suddenly stopped and checked her watch once again.

"Stay here and don't move. I'll be back shortly." She barely glanced at them as she continued forward alone.

For a moment, they stood quietly and watched her walk out of sight. Maggie leaned against a nearby tree, relieved to have a moment to rest. Her legs ached from their pace.

"So, how long have you worked for the Resistance?" Ryker asked casually, though the way his eyes glared at Wick, Maggie knew it was anything but.

He laughed. "I don't work for them. It's more like we

indulge each other when we have to."

"What does that mean?" His tone was not friendly. Maggie glanced from him back to Wick. They stood only a few yards apart, neither relaxed and both on guard. "Don't you believe in the cause?"

"You mean, do I think the act should be repealed? Of course. Do I agree with the Resistance's tactics? Not a chance. The longer you're around them, the more you'll know what I mean. You shouldn't put so much faith in them."

"They do what is necessary. They've been bringing me up-to-speed on everything. I only wish I'd been able to do something sooner," Ryker said.

"Have they? What exactly have they told you?" Wick crossed his arms. Despite Ryker's judgmental tone, he remained calm and even had a small smirk on his face.

"Quite a few things. The most impressive was when they put some people undercover as Remos." Maggie looked at him, surprised. He turned toward her as he continued. "They were able to tip off the Resistance of an impending raid in the city. The Resistance moved everyone out and, in their place, they set up an ambush. They killed four Remos, and none of the illegals were taken. Man, I wish I could've been a part of that."

Wick tilted his head. "Did they tell you what happened to the guys undercover?"

Ryker looked at him and their eyes locked. Neither looked away.

"No? Well, the DRM knew someone had tipped off the Resistance, so they interrogated each of the surviving Remos – interrogated them hard. Finally, they found the two spies. Their blood was taken and run through the system. Each family member of the two men, anyone they could find, was taken. Some were in prisons, centers, illegals; some were normal folks on the street. It didn't matter. They were all taken. Killed. Only after it was done were the spies themselves killed and their bodies were dumped at the site of the ambush."

"The public would never allow innocent people to be murdered like that." Maggie shook her head.

"You're right, they wouldn't allow it. If they knew about it. Do you really think the DRM doesn't have that kind of reach?"

"If the undercover guys were killed, how do you know any of that?" Ryker crossed his arms

"The Resistance ran blood tests on both men, wanting to notify their families about what happened. That's when they found out."

"But the Resistance didn't intend for that to happen. They never would've allowed the mission to—"

"To what? To go forward?" Wick's arms uncrossed as he unconsciously stepped forward and his tone hardened stiffly. "After the ambush, the Resistance made those two men go back to the DRM. They told them they had to remain undercover, or else they would expose them themselves. Those men had no choice.

They were murdered by the Resistance."

Ryker laughed. "And how do you know they told them that?"

"Because... I've been around for a while." Wick shook his head and walked away from them.

Ryker glanced at Maggie and rolled his eyes. She didn't respond. She could see something dark lurking in Wick's eyes. Knowing the tragic past that she and her brother carried, she wondered what exactly he'd been through. Regardless, she suddenly found it easier to believe him. That wasn't the look of someone unsure of himself.

+ + +

"We need to move fast." Morrigan appeared abruptly in front of them.

"To where?" Ryker asked.

She didn't answer. She merely turned and moved back into the woods. They begrudgingly followed, but after only a short distance, Morrigan stopped. She waved at them to get close together, and despite the earlier tension, they crammed shoulder-to-shoulder next to her.

"Just down there is the fence." Morrigan pointed in front of them. Squinting her eyes, Maggie could just make it out through the foliage. "At the base of the fence, there's a weak point we've created where people can crawl underneath." She stared at her watch as she spoke. "When I give the word, we need to move as fast as possible. We'll only have a few short minutes to get everyone across. Do you understand?"

They all nodded.

Heavy silence sat over them as they waited. Each second felt like an hour until, suddenly, Morrigan hissed, "Now!"

She ran to the fence. Maggie couldn't see any weak point as they sprinted behind her. The fence towered above them as the perfect, solid structure it was, and she feared Morrigan was in the wrong place. But their leader dropped to her knees and dug her fingers into the dirt and grass. She pulled upward, and immediately, the ground itself gave way. What had appeared to be part of the earth was nothing more than a cleverly disguised cover that hid an opening no bigger than an average person.

Morrigan shoved her upper body into the hole and the ground on the other side of the fence popped up. She pulled herself back and waved at them. "Move!"

Ryker threw himself on the ground and wormed his way into the tight space. Maggie was certain her brother's broad shoulders would never fit, but in seconds, he was on the other side.

Wick grabbed her hand. "You next."

She nodded and followed Ryker's lead. The earth was cold against her body. Dirt fell on her with every moment, sending shivers down her spine at the thought of the tunnel collapsing, but she forced her fear down. As sunlight hit her face, Ryker's hand clamped on her wrist and he pulled her forcefully into the fresh air.

"Make for the tree line. We'll be right behind you," Morrigan instructed.

Without hesitating, Ryker dragged Maggie toward the tree line and she struggled to pull free of his grip. Right as they reached the edge of the woods, she managed to shove him away and turn back to the border. She had to know Wick made it across safely.

He was crouched down, helping Morrigan slide the last tunnel cover back into place. Within seconds, there was no trace they'd ever been there. Wick and Morrigan ran toward the woods, but even as they reach them, their guide didn't slow. Without a word, she continued further and further through the trees, looking at her watch every few seconds. They moved forward in this manner for almost half an hour, and Maggie could feel exhaustion beginning to take its toll. She needed a break.

"Morrigan, don't you think—"

"Quiet."

She exhaled loudly. "No, this is ridiculous. I'm not—"

Morrigan turned toward her so sharply it caught her off guard. "If you don't want to be arrested, I suggest you shut up and follow me."

Anger burned in Maggie's chest, however, she resisted the urge to respond. The unfortunate truth was that she didn't know if they were really in danger in their current position. For all she knew, they were in the middle of nowhere, then again, there could be a DRM station just fifteen yards further into the woods.

Another twenty minutes passed before they came to a small dirt road. Morrigan walked to the edge of the tree line to what appeared to be a large bush, then she began pulling branches off and throwing them to the ground. It was several seconds before Maggie realized it was fake foliage that was hiding a dark green SUV. The three companions helped uncover their transportation, each feeling relieved once safely inside. Ryker and Maggie sat in the back of the SUV, with Wick sitting in the passenger seat – as runners, they still had to keep the two of them as concealed as possible.

"Why was timing so tight getting across?" Maggie asked.

"You expect it to be easy?" Morrigan didn't take her eyes off the road.

"I'm curious about why you said we only had a few minutes. If we had taken any longer, what would've happened?"

"The motion detectors would've seen us. When we need to cross, we hack into the system and shut down all the sensors along the border. All they have to do is reboot the system to get it back online, and that only takes about four minutes. Most times, anyway."

"Most times?"

"Obviously, it's a big flaw in the system. They know when the sensors go down that illegals are jumping a border, but it's too large of a space to send Remos to every section. They've been working to upgrade the programming and we've found the reboot time is getting shorter and shorter. Pretty soon, it'll be mere seconds at best."

"How do you know we had the full four minutes?" Ryker asked.

"I don't. For all I know, they saw us, hence why we need to get out of here as soon as possible." Morrigan continued down the dirt road, and even as they hit the pavement, they stayed to the back lanes. Maggie opened her mouth to respond, but then stopped. She took a deep breath and looked out the window. Despite their situation, she couldn't help but smile. They had successfully made it across one border, which left only three more to go. It'd only been a few hours since they'd left the Resistance in Michigan. If they kept their current pace, she'd meet her uncle by the end of the day. The day couldn't end fast enough.

Chapter Sixteen

"Maggie, wake up." Ryker nudged her arm. Her eyes shot open as her heart raced. They were still in the SUV. "We're almost at the border."

She nodded and rubbed her eyes. They were on a small road surrounded by cornfields and farmhouses. No other cars were in sight. Suddenly, Morrigan took a sharp left turn into an opening so narrow and hidden within one of the cornfields that Maggie would never have noticed it.

"We have to go the rest of the way on foot." Morrigan pulled the vehicle to a stop, turned off the ignition and got out.

It wasn't easy to move through the corn. Despite trying to avoid it, Maggie got hit by stalk after stalk as they walked, and little cuts marked her arms as she tried to protect her face. A thick row of trees and bushes sat at the end of the field. She hoped there was an easy way through but was soon disappointed as they pushed and pulled their way into the thicket.

Morrigan stopped on the other side, knelt down and waved for them to do the same. She looked at her watch again and her jaw tightened. Minutes passed, and the frequency at which she checked her watch began to annoy Maggie. It was only putting them more on edge. Suddenly, a black SUV came tumbling down the dirt road in front of them. Her heart leapt to her throat, but Morrigan merely sighed. The SUV came to an abrupt halt, and with the engine still running, the driver got out.

Morrigan walked forward. "Where the hell have you been?"

"I'm here, aren't I?" The man held an odd presence. He was much shorter than both Wick and Ryker, though still taller than Maggie herself. His hair was light, peppered with grey and what had before been black. Wrinkles lined his eyes and forehead, making him appear much older than he otherwise would have. Yet, he looked tough, almost dangerous. It was obvious the man had seen a lot, and it'd only hardened him.

"You were meant to be here twenty minutes ago. The timing was set up for a reason!" She looked back at them and rolled her eyes. "Let's go!"

They glanced at each other and stepped forward.

"I thought there were only two?" He eyed them all suspiciously.

"Yeah, well, you don't like rules anyway." Morrigan

pointed at the man as she turned toward them. "This is Victor Blackwood. He'll get you across the Ohio-Pennsylvania border and then pass you along to your next contact, who'll take you from there."

"I don't take stowaways," he said, rubbing his chin and looking between Ryker and Wick. "So, which of you is staying behind?"

Both boys opened their mouths simultaneously, but Maggie stepped forward between them.

"Neither of them."

"Listen, darling, you don't—"

"They're both coming with us. That's not negotiable, Victor." His eyes narrowed, but she held his gaze.

He glanced at Morrigan, who smirked slightly, and then back to Maggie. "First of all, it's Blackwood. Second, let's get something straight – I'm in charge here. If I say I'm taking two of you, I'm taking two. Got it?"

"Then the three of us are going on without you."

"Maggie, knock it off," Ryker said.

She turned on him as the frustration of the last few hours took hold. "No. So far, Wick has had more insight into what's going on than you or me. I'm not leaving him behind, not unless he wants to be left."

"Keep your voices down." Morrigan looked at her watch yet again. "You need to get moving."

Blackwood looked from her to Wick, finally determining who was the extra among them. "You can come along, but I'm not responsible for you. I agreed to take two. Should something happen, you're on your own."

"Fine."

Morrigan gave them a curt nod as she made her way back through the thicket alone. Maggie and Ryker slid into the backseat, once again leaving the front for Wick. As Blackwood calmly climbed behind the wheel, he stared uncomfortably at Wick. He took out a cigarette and lit it, allowing silence to invade the small space as he took a long drag.

"So, how was your morning with Morrigan?" He glanced back at Maggie.

"It was…quick." She tried to be positive.

He laughed. "Yeah, she's not the most personable of us railroaders, but she has a particularly hard job."

"How's that?" Ryker asked.

"The Michigan-Ohio border is one of the toughest in the country to cross."

"It seemed pretty easy actually," Maggie said.

"That's because you're not smart enough to know how dangerous it really was."

Heat pulsed in her chest. "And what's so dangerous about it?"

Blackwood took another long drag and blew even more smoke through the cabin. "Don't you kids know anything? Any border state is damn near impossible to get into, because then you're only one line away from freedom. It's not often that runners are trying to get further into the country." He stubbed his cigarette out on the dash and threw the butt out the window. He turned to look directly at Maggie and Ryker. "So, why is it that you are?"

"We're trying to find our family," Maggie said.

Blackwood stared at them for a moment before turning forward again. Without another word, he put the SUV in gear and slowly pulled back down the road.

"How far until we have to walk across the next border?" Ryker asked.

Blackwood chuckled. "Walk across? I don't do that. We're driving."

"How are we supposed to do that?"

"You'll be sitting comfortably in the trunk compartment, and I'll do the talking out here." He glanced at Wick. "Not sure I can fit the three of you in there. One of you will probably be crossing over with me."

"Not a problem," Wick said. "I can sit up front."

"I'll tell them I picked you up hitchhiking, hopefully they won't search us too closely." Blackwood eyed him for a reaction.

"Don't worry. I've reprogrammed my ID. If they scan it, we'll be fine."

He snorted and shook his head. "It's your neck."

"You do know they have infrared and body-heat detection capabilities, right?" Ryker asked.

Blackwood sighed. "Son, I've been doing this a long

time. Of course, I know that. The compartment has a special lining to make it through their little tricks."

"How does—"

"Call it whatever you want. Can we just stop with all the questions?" He rubbed his temple.

They drove forward in uncomfortable silence. Maggie expected to get to a real road, anything that would indicate a greater level of civilization, but they stayed on the narrow, back lanes. The only thing that could be seen for miles was farmland and the random houses or barns attached to it.

"The border is just a few more miles down the road. You two need to get into the compartment," Blackwood said. As he drove, he pulled a folded paper from the inner pocket of his jacket. His eyes darted between the road and the document as he carefully scribbled on it.

Maggie and Ryker looked at each other, neither sure where he was talking about.

"Compartment?" she asked. The SUV continued to sail down the road at an unbelievable rate.

Blackwood sighed. "There's a cup holder on the floor between you. Pull it out, and hit the button underneath."

They both looked down and saw two standard cup holders. Ryker grabbed them and pulled, but nothing happened.

"Put some strength behind it," Blackwood said, amused.

Ryker grinded his teeth and pulled hard with both

hands. The plastic insert shot free, revealing a small, blue button. Maggie pushed it and a hushed pop came from the trunk of the SUV. Looking behind their seat, she saw the floor standing slightly ajar. Together, they grabbed the edge and lifted it up. The metal door creaked painfully as it gave way to reveal the dark compartment.

"Hurry it up, we're almost there."

Maggie took a deep breath as she maneuvered over the back seat and lowered herself in. The metal was cold against her skin, sending shivers through her body. She pulled her jacket up as high as it would go around her neck, but still, the chill was there. She pushed her body further into the compartment, sliding under the back seat, and watched as Ryker followed her movements and settled in beside her.

"Ready?" His hands were on the door.

She nodded, and he pulled it shut, sealing out the light. The releases clicked back into place and locked them in. Maggie prayed there was an emergency release somewhere in the dark hole, though she knew if there were, it would be near impossible to find. Her heart was starting to beat faster as the darkness and cold settled in around her. Suddenly, a hand wrapped around hers.

"It's going to be ok," Ryker said.

She nodded. "I know."

As the vehicle continued forward, they bumped painfully against the metal and Maggie was forced to brace her hands against the door to try to stop her body from slamming up and down. Her arms started to relax as the vehicle slowed, though her heart sped up. *This must be it.* They waited in silence, straining to hear anything.

"Good morning, sir. ID please." The voice was deep and rigid.

"I don't have one."

Maggie was surprised by how easily she could hear Blackwood. She held her breath, realizing sound could travel both ways.

"You don't have one?"

"Sonny, look at me. I'm as old as six feet of dirt. You really think after living all these years without one of those pieces of metal under my skin, I'd just run right out and get one?"

"Sir, you are required—"

"No, I'm not. I'm over fifty, so I don't need one. I know the law, champ. Here's my permit to go back and forth over the border. We do this all day long for our company, so you better get used to seeing my charming face." Blackwood was both condescending and firm.

"Troy Insurance? You're telling me that Ohio and Pennsylvania don't have their own insurance companies?"

"Ones as good as us? Unlikely." Blackwood laughed.

"Sir, I'd appreciate short, direct answers. Otherwise, I am authorized to detain you until all my questions have been thoroughly answered."

His laughter immediately stopped. "You could do that. But you should keep in mind that Troy has offices all across the country, each responsible for a specific territory. As it is in many states, the west Pennsylvania office, in which we work, also covers the eastern fringe of Ohio. This is because it's hard to find people that are qualified and willing to drive all over kingdom come just to be harassed by kids working the border. And then on top of it, yelled at by people whose insurance doesn't cover *that* type of accident."

"Sir—"

"You should also be aware that because Troy is such a large corporation, they have a full team of lawyers at their disposal. They even handle employee harassment by border control. Now, sonny, my paperwork is in order, so you have no legal right to hold us here. Do you really want me to have to call my attorney?"

"You might have the proper paperwork, but what about him?"

"I—" Wick started.

"This young man is a new trainee, and as you can see in my permit, he is also authorized."

"You look pretty young. I'm sure you have an ID. Let's see it."

"Of course. Just so you know, today is my first day. I can't promise they've uploaded my new job information. I only finished the paperwork this morning," Wick said.

"That's why we have the permit to begin with,"

Blackwood growled. Maggie could hear the anger in his voice. If she didn't know better, she would've easily believed him.

Silence took the small space, and she strained to hear any indication of what was happening. Minutes seemed to drag by. It might have only been a few seconds, but it was impossible to determine.

"You're clear to go, but next time, try to keep your attitude to a minimum. You'll make it through with fewer problems."

"Sure thing, sonny."

The SUV lurched forward. Maggie felt so much relief that she didn't even notice the painful jostling. Even as the vehicle picked up speed, neither she nor Ryker spoke, and their breathing was quiet in the tight space. Suddenly, the compartment popped open, letting in the outside light. Maggie squinted as Wick came into view smiling.

"Welcome to Pennsylvania."

Chapter Seventeen

After successfully making it across the border, Maggie felt even more hopeful their trip would be completed without incident. She knew it would be difficult, but she allowed her mind to imagine what it would be like to sneak across the country undetected. Still, despite her hopeful excitement, she couldn't avoid the awkwardness of the car ride. Blackwood drove in uncomfortable silence, and the only sound came from his index finger tapping over and over against the steering wheel.

"How long until the next border?" she asked.

Immediately, the tapping stopped. "Aren't we excited to cross another one? You know they're not all going to be that easy, darling," Blackwood said tauntingly.

"My second border in less than three hours, I think I know that. How long?"

"A few hours," Wick said, looking at the map on his phone.

"Right." Knowing the snide remarks she'd have to endure with further conversation, she turned toward the window and closed her eyes, but even though she was exhausted, she couldn't sleep. Ryker and Wick began to argue once again, as if her sleeping gave them permission. The argument centered on who was making the best decisions for them, or rather, who was in charge to make those decisions. Surprisingly, Blackwood stayed quiet and joined in only to egg on the discussion when it seemed it might finally die down.

Finally, not being able to take it anymore, she opened her eyes. Wick was turned completely around and staring angrily at Ryker, who was leaning forward and returning the same look. In spite of being restrained by their seatbelts, the two boys were only a foot from one another. Ryker had removed his shoulder harness, allowing him to get closer with each exchange.

Maggie exhaled sharply as she looked from the boys to Blackwood. His head sagged low and his arms hung from the steering wheel. From where she sat, his body looked completely defeated. As her eyes came back to Wick, she saw the car in front of them slam on its brakes. Her heart leapt to her throat as she realized they weren't slowing.

"Look out!" she screamed.

Blackwood shuddered, and he jerked the steering wheel hard to the right. It was too late. They clipped the back of the vehicle in front of them, sending them spinning into the next lane. The tires squealed angrily against the pavement, and though Maggie tried to hold herself steady, the spinning was so forceful she lost her grip. Something smashed hard against the rear of the vehicle, and they all felt a sudden weightlessness as they flew into the air. Maggie's breath caught in her throat. She hung suspended for a moment and then crashed violently against the pavement.

+ + +

"Are you all right? Can you hear me?" The voice was muffled. Slowly, Maggie opened her eyes. Her head pounded relentlessly, making the smallest movement a struggle. She was in the SUV, but it was all wrong. She was upside down.

"Answer me!" It was Blackwood.

"I'm...I'm ok." Her voice was weak. Looking to her left, she could see her brother strapped in beside her. "Ryker?"

He didn't respond. She pushed her body toward him to get a better look at his face. His eyes were closed. Blood dripped in a thick stream down his forehead to the roof below, making a sick *tick-tick* sound. The seatbelt restricted her movement so she couldn't quite reach him.

Maggie grabbed the passenger seat in front of her and used her right arm to steady her body in place. Her muscles were stiff and resisted the motion. The noises around her were deafening – someone was screaming in the distance, other people were shouting, an odd hissing came from the vehicle itself, and all this was made worse by the pounding in her head. She took a deep breath and pressed her seatbelt loose.

Her wedged position held for only a second before her hand slipped from the passenger seat. Maggie fell hard to the bottom of the overturned SUV, smashing into broken glass and protruding metal that brutally cut into her palms and forearms. She tried to inch carefully through the wreck, but each movement dug the glass in deeper.

"Give me your hand." Blackwood appeared outside the broken window next to her.

She glanced back at Ryker, who still hung silently behind her, and then back to him. "No, I have to get Ryker out of here."

Blackwood snatched her arm and prevented her from moving further into the ruined SUV. "You're not going to do any good from in there. Now move."

The force in his voice jolted her forward. She put her right hand in his and ordered her body to crawl from the wreckage. He pulled her out, though his crushing grip pushed the glass in her palm even deeper. She emerged and the bright light of the sun immediately invaded her senses, making it more difficult to think.

"Are you all right?" Blackwood's shadow fell over her

face as he shifted to inspect her injuries.

She nodded. "I'm fine. We have to get Ryker out of there." She forced her mind to move past the pain. "Where's Wick?"

Blackwood glanced at the overturned vehicle and, without a word, he walked to the other side where Ryker was still suspended. Maggie pulled herself to her feet and went to the passenger side window. Her heart raced as she crouched down and saw Wick's body hanging limp from the seat.

She dropped to the ground beside the window. "Get Ryker out. I'll help Wick."

Blackwood didn't respond, but she took his silence as agreement. Despite the extensive damage to the vehicle, the passenger side window was still intact. She leaned back on the cement, and as she held herself steady, she kicked the glass with all her strength. Each blow sent painful vibrations up her leg, but she struck the glass over and over until it finally shattered inward.

"Wick? Can you hear me?" She crawled into the vehicle and lightly touched his cheek. "Wick?"

His head moved at her touch, followed by a groan. She sighed as his eyes slowly fluttered open.

"What happened?"

"There was an accident. Are you ok?"

"I think so."

"Give me your arm."

Maggie got on her feet, forcing her body into a

painful crouched position, then shoved her shoulder under his armpit. He grunted but wrapped his arm around her shoulder without a word.

"When I count to three, hit the seatbelt release and try to use your legs to guide your body down."

Wick laughed. "When you say it like that, how hard can it be?"

She forced a smile. "Here we go. One…two…three."

He clicked the release button and his body crashed hard on top of her, knocking her painfully to her back. She started laughing, knowing how ridiculous that must have looked.

"I'm so sorry," he said as their eyes met, and he tried to push himself off of her.

"It's all right. Can you move?"

He nodded. He looked at the broken passenger window and then ahead to the driver's window. "I think it'll be easier to go through the driver's side. Don't move. I don't want to accidentally step on you."

She nodded and held as still as possible. Wick crawled over her, his body hovering only inches above hers as he went until, finally, he pulled himself free from the tangled mess. As carefully as she could, she rolled onto her stomach and followed his same path. Wick's outstretched hand waited for hers as she maneuvered through the broken glass, and it was a welcome sight.

In the bright light, she could see how pale he was. Small scrapes lined the right side of his face, but otherwise, he looked unscathed.

"Are you all right?" she asked.

He nodded slowly, but immediately stopped as his hand shot to his neck. "I'm fine. My neck is just really stiff, but it's no big deal." He reached out and touched her cheek, causing her stomach to flutter while also sending sharp pain down her face. "Are you ok? This cut looks pretty deep."

Maggie hadn't realized she'd been hurt. She lightly touched where he was indicating and was surprised to pull back two fingers covered in blood. She wiped her fingers clean and shook her head.

"It's nothing." She turned just as Blackwood pulled Ryker's body from the backseat. Her heart stopped as she finally saw her brother in clear light.

The entire left side of his face was covered in blood from a large gash running the length of his face. Maggie ran over to get a closer look, fearing she could be looking at his lifeless body.

"Please tell me he's still alive," she said.

Blackwood rubbed the back of his neck. "He's alive." He went to the back of the SUV and crawled into the trunk. He was gone for only a second before appearing with one of their backpacks in hand. He silently dug through until he pulled out a small medical kit.

Maggie and Wick watched as he cleaned the wound and hastily wrapped bandages around it, finally closing the grotesque opening. "That'll keep him until an ambulance gets here." He shoved the remaining supplies back in the pack.

"An ambulance?" She looked at the carnage around them. Several damaged and broken vehicles surrounded theirs. Six in total. People were screaming and yelling for help for loved ones, all while those that were spared the accident looked on in horror. "The cops will come before an ambulance. We can't be here when they do."

"That's right. If we're here when they start showing up, it'll only be a matter of time before we're all arrested. Especially when they realize the car crossed the border with two people and is now carrying four." Blackwood nodded grimly.

"Then you need to fix him up so we can move him," Maggie said, glancing at Wick for support. His face was dark as he watched Blackwood's every move.

"Sorry, darling, but we're leaving him here. He'll slow us down too much, and we can't risk it."

"Slow us down?" Fury pulsed in her chest.

"What do you think those cops are going to do when they get here and realize there are people unaccounted for? They'll know we're runners or illegals or any number of criminals. Our blood is all over the inside of the truck. You think they won't run it and get those answers?" Blackwood stood up, and she immediately did the same, bringing them face-to-face.

"I think that all takes time. Enough time to get Ryker out of here."

"I'd think you'd be concerned about your brother living more than anything else. He needs a doctor."

"If they take him to the hospital, they'll run a blood test. He'll be back in DRM custody within a few hours," Wick said.

Maggie rubbed her face as she tried to think. There was no way of knowing how bad his injuries were, and if left untreated, what would happen, but she feared what Hayden would do if he got a hold of him.

"You know fully well that he wouldn't want to be taken back into custody, regardless of what's in his best interest," Wick continued.

"Then, by all means, let's drag him into the woods to die." Blackwood rolled his eyes.

Her eyes shot from Blackwood to her brother as her mind whirled. The pounding in her head was making it difficult to think. Wick grabbed her hand, bringing her focus to him. "What would you want to do? If it was you?"

She half smiled, knowing he was right. "I'd want to keep going."

"Once they call the Remos in, they'll be after us faster than a dog with a scent. We don't have time to be carrying dead weight." Blackwood paced impatiently as he looked from them to the growing crowd just beyond the wreckage. He pulled a small blue box from his pocket, put it to his lips, and inhaled. Maggie looked at Wick whose jaw tightened at the sight, but she ignored it, forcing herself to focus on her brother.

"We're not—"

"Listen, darling, I was given one task. That was to get you to the New York border, not all these tagalongs you brought with you. It's unfortunate to lose someone committed to the cause, but it is what it is." As he spoke, Blackwood slid his arms through the backpack's straps and threw the second to Wick.

Maggie looked at Wick, horrified at what was happening. He looked down at the backpack in his hands, glancing from her to Blackwood, then he sighed as his gaze finally settled on Ryker. He took a deep breath and handed her the bag.

"We're not leaving him behind," Wick said. "I'll carry him."

Blackwood laughed. "He weighs as much as you do, sonny. You won't last ten minutes."

Wick knelt in front of Ryker and lightly tapped his face, but there was no response. He sighed again. "Help me get him up."

Maggie immediately grabbed one of her brother's arms. Wick followed on the other side and, together, they wrenched him to a sitting position.

"You have to be kidding if—"

"We're not leaving him behind, so you might as well be quiet," Maggie snapped.

Blackwood's eyes narrowed. Without warning, he grabbed her shoulder and pushed her away from

Ryker, sending her crouched body to her knees. She sprung up as rage burst through her veins, but stopped as Blackwood, together with Wick, pulled Ryker to a standing position.

"This is a mistake," he mumbled as he positioned his shoulder under Ryker's arm.

The crowd of onlookers stared as they made their way off the road, and voices shouted for them to wait for an ambulance. None of them looked back. Blackwood and Wick grunted and wheezed as they dragged Ryker to the top of the steep hill that led into the woods.

"We need to find some cover." Blackwood's eyes shot around as sirens grew louder in the distance. "There."

His eyes were locked on several large boulders clustered together. The tight spaces between them were difficult to maneuver between. They stood just feet from a drop off that left anyone with a thirty-foot fall should they slip. They positioned Ryker behind the largest one, though his feet were forced to dangle slightly off the edge.

"What's going on?" Ryker whispered suddenly.

Maggie knelt beside him as his eyes slowly opened. "There was an accident."

"My head is killing me." He tried to move but she pushed his shoulders down.

"Stay still. The police are—"

"Darling, are you trying to get us killed?" Blackwood hissed. "Get back!"

She realized the boulder that was concealing her brother did not cover her. She turned around right as Wick grabbed her arm and pulled her behind the next boulder. There was barely enough space for the two of them, forcing their bodies tight against one another. She could feel her face grow warm as they held still.

"How long until we can move?" she whispered.

"The police won't search for long, not when they have the others to deal with, but once they run the blood from the car, there'll be Remos after us," he answered.

They sat in silence and waited for a sign that they could safely move. Maggie drifted off but was soon startled awake by nearing voices. Police. Wick grabbed her hand as she tried to turn to see their faces. He shook his head and held his finger to his lips. She nodded and nudged in closer to him, suddenly fearful the boulder wasn't providing enough cover. Glancing at Ryker, she could see his eyes were open, but he didn't move. Blackwood was just beyond her brother, but he was focused, seemingly ready to pounce should there be any need for it.

"We know you're out here. Please come in! You need medical attention!" The voice boomed through the woods, but the sound bounced off the trees, making it impossible to determine just how close they were.

"You will not be placed under arrest! We're not interested in who you are!" A second voice shouted, equally as loud.

A branch snapped only feet from where they were hidden. Maggie's heart raced. She glanced at Ryker and he shook his head, telling her not to move. Another branch snapped. They were close. She felt a sudden urge to run, but she knew it wasn't an option, not with Ryker's injuries, and she would not abandon him. She took a deep breath, although it did nothing to calm her racing heart. Another branch snapped. She closed her eyes, trying to block out everything around her, and willed the footsteps to retreat.

Another branch snapped.

Chapter Eighteen

"We need to move." Blackwood stood as he spoke, his eyes fixated on the woods behind them.

His voice startled Maggie, breaking the silence for the first time in what seemed like hours. The police had come dangerously close, but they hadn't looked beyond the boulders. Still, none of them felt safe. She glanced at Wick, suddenly aware of how much she was invading his space. It somehow seemed more obvious now that secrecy wasn't their top priority. More abruptly than intended, she pushed herself away. Wick's eyebrows rose, however, he remained silent as he stood.

"Do you know where we're going?" Ryker asked.

Maggie crawled over to him. "How are you feeling?"

"I'm fine." His eyes were glassy and it was easy to see his head still hurt.

She kneeled forward to get a closer look at his head.

The bandages were soaked with blood, but from the state of drying, it appeared the bleeding had stopped.

Maggie grabbed her backpack and dug through it until, finally, she found more bandages. She carefully removed the old dressing and cleaned the wound as much as she dared before reapplying a fresh bandage. Ryker winced but didn't protest. His attention was focused on their other companions.

"I know where we are." Blackwood continued to scan the horizon.

Wick pulled his phone out and looked at the map. "It's hard to pinpoint our exact position in the woods, but based on the last mile marker I saw, I'd say we're in this area." He pointed to the map. Blackwood glanced at him and smiled.

"I don't need a device telling me where I am, sonny."

"You just happen to know exactly where we are? Spend a lot of time in these woods?" He shoved his phone into his pocket.

"The more important question is, can we walk from here?" Maggie asked.

"Anything's possible, darling, but it's going to take a while. It's a long distance to cover," Blackwood said before adding, "and I hate walking."

"Is there another car we could pick up? We're not walking from here. That's ridiculous," Ryker said.

"Not nearby, and it's not like we can just go to the nearest town and call someone up. That's the first place the Remos are going to look. We're on our own."

"No, what we need to do is—" Ryker started.

"Listen, consider yourself lucky that you're even with us right now. If it wasn't for your sister, that wouldn't be the case. We're walking. You don't like it, don't come."

Ryker's face blazed red but Blackwood ignored it as he moved further into the woods. Maggie glanced uncomfortably at her brother as she followed him. Wick was right that the DRM would test their blood. It was obvious they were fugitives, and when they discovered who they were, they'd be coming. As Blackwood put it, runners were always top priorities. They didn't want the general population to know that kids at the centers felt a need to escape. And in their particular case, Maggie had a strong suspicion they would be an even higher priority.

Their pace was slow as they walked single file with Blackwood leading, Wick behind him, then Ryker, and Maggie at the end. She wanted to be last, or at least behind her brother in order to keep a closer eye on him. She could see him struggling to maintain his balance, and he used tree after tree for support. As they maneuvered down a steep hill, his hand slipped from a tree he was leaning on, causing him to fall forward. She lunged, grabbing his shirt and stopping him from tumbling down.

"Are you all right?"

"Fine." He pushed her hands away as she tried to help him up.

"Maybe we should take a break. You don't look fine."

"We can hold up here for a second," Wick offered.

"No, I'm good." He tried to keep moving, but Maggie grabbed his arm.

"Ryker—"

He whipped around and stepped so close she was forced to take a step back. "If I want your help, I'll ask for it. In case you've forgotten, I can take care of myself."

"I just want to make sure you're ok." The loathing in his eyes startled her.

"No, you're just relishing the fact that for once I didn't save you."

"What?"

"Every time something bad happens, I'm there to get you out. I stopped your transfer, I stopped Hayden when he attacked you, I stopped those Remos from arresting us – I'm the one that always bails us out." He rolled his eyes. "And you're the one the Resistance needs."

Maggie stood frozen as rage built inside of her. She didn't rely on him. They relied on each other. "You know that's not true."

"Enough. We need to keep moving," Blackwood said without turning back to look at them. He was several yards ahead and still moving down the hill.

Ryker grinded his teeth as he turned toward him.

"Keep moving to where? I've had enough of just wandering behind you like an idiot. Where are you taking us?"

Blackwood didn't stop, nor did he look back. Ryker

grunted as he charged down the hill.

"I'm talking to you! I want some answers!"

"Knock it off." Maggie's temper was on edge, and though she wasn't sure how she felt about their surly guide, she didn't like the way her brother was speaking to him. He'd gotten them that far, and despite wanting to, he didn't leave Ryker behind.

Ryker maneuvered down the hill, sliding on leaves as he went, until he finally reached Blackwood. He grabbed his arm and pulled him back with a harsh jerk. "I'm sick of your games, old man! I want some answers!"

Blackwood shoved the hand from his arm. "If you don't want to follow me, then don't. No one's making you. If you're looking for answers, find a book. I don't answer to sniveling brats."

He turned away and continued down the hill. Maggie was near to her brother when he tackled Blackwood, sending them both tumbling violently down the steep incline. Her breath caught in her throat as she watched them fall. The sounds of cracking branches and angered grunts vibrated through the woods. Their bodies slammed into a large tree branch, trapping Ryker's leg in its crux and leaving Blackwood to fall the remaining way on his own. It was only a few seconds more before he hit the bottom with a loud thud.

For a moment, neither Wick nor Maggie moved, but they were pushed into action when Ryker grunted in pain as he tried to free his leg. They rushed down the hill and reached him just as he was able to pull it free.

"Are you all right?" she asked, looking from his face to his leg. Wick glanced at them silently as he made his way down to Blackwood.

Ryker nodded, though she could see the pain was genuine. Peering down the hill, Wick halted as Blackwood moved – he was climbing back up. Determination pulsed in his eyes. Maggie jumped to her feet and stepped in front of her brother right as he got to them.

"Get out of the way," he growled.

"No. It's over." She held her hands out in front of her, creating a barrier between the two.

Blackwood grabbed her wrist and tried to pull her out of the way, but Maggie lowered her shoulder into his chest. He slid a few feet down the hill as he tried to maintain his balance on the slippery leaves.

"We have more important things to do than worry about you two fighting." She threw a scathing look from the old man to her brother. "Ryker, you have no better idea of where we are right now than anyone else, so keep your opinions to yourself. Blackwood, try to keep your name calling to a minimum. It only makes things worse. Got it?"

Wick smirked and looked away.

"Fine," Ryker mumbled as he pulled himself to his feet.

"Yeah, all right, darling. But if that kid tries something

like that again, no amount of heartfelt words are going to save him. You got it?"

Maggie gave a brisk nod. They all made their way down in silence. Glancing at her brother, she could still see the same hate and anger in his eyes. She wondered if he was at all sorry for what he'd said to her. Just thinking of it sent rage back into her chest, but she pushed it down. She knew something else was bothering him, something dark, and it was only a matter of time before it came out.

Chapter Nineteen

Two more days passed in the same rhythm. They would trek for miles, pausing only for rare breaks, and eventually stopped for the night in crudely constructed camps. Blackwood barely spoke, and when he did, it was an order grunted forcefully. Occasionally, Maggie noticed him inhaling from the same small, blue box, but she resisted the urge to ask about it, fearing the answer would only cause another argument. Ryker spoke even less, and the tension between the two was almost unbearable.

"Get close behind me," Blackwood ordered suddenly as they reached the end of their third day. "If we approach too fast, we could get shot."

"Approach what too fast?" Maggie asked.

As usual, he didn't respond. Her heart raced. In her mind, she hoped it was the border, though she knew logically they still had a long way to go.

It was late in the day, and combined with the thick

treetops above, the woods were getting dark. It was difficult to make out what they were advancing toward. Blackwood stopped, holding his hand up to make sure they did as well. Birds chirped in the distance, echoing through the forest, and leaves rustled against the wind, but there were no other sounds. He started moving again, but slower and more cautiously. They continued for nearly forty yards until a community appeared in front of them.

"Who the hell – Blackwood. I should have known." A clean-shaven man in his mid-forties came toward them. "You could've been killed."

"I know how to get into this camp, despite however many people you have on watch." Blackwood seemed amused.

"Who're the tagalongs?"

"Part of the Resistance. We need a car. We're trying to get to the border and we're already days behind schedule."

"What is this place?" Maggie could see tent after tent with people everywhere. There were men, women, and children, and yet the large group was surprisingly quiet. There was no boisterous talking, no echoing laughter, or children running. These people were used to hiding.

"It's a Resistance camp, what's it look like?" Blackwood answered. They made their way further into the camp and away from the tree line.

"We'll have to talk to Lenkin. See what we can do."

Their new guide glanced at them. "Why don't they get some supper? Looks like you haven't fed them in weeks. Then you and I can talk."

"We don't need to be put at the kid's table," Ryker said.

"We need to know what's going on," Maggie agreed.

Blackwood held her stare but sighed. "Trust me, they're impossible to get rid of. Let's go. We don't have all day."

The man led them through the camp. People stopped and stared as they went, and it was obvious that visitors were not common. Finally, they came to a tent in the center of the camp that was much larger than all the others. As they entered, Maggie couldn't help but think of the last time they were brought to meet the leaders of a Resistance camp. She took a deep breath.

"Blackwood, as I live and breathe. I was certain you must be dead by now." A man stepped forward from a group that was crowded around a table. It seemed planning and scheming were commonplace among these types of people.

"You can wish it all you want, Lenkin, but I'm still here." Blackwood smiled. The men embraced tightly and Maggie and Wick glanced at one another.

"What's with the kids?"

"No time to explain. We lost our truck and need a new one. What have you got?"

"Nothing I can spare." Lenkin stared at Maggie,

studying her face. She shifted uncomfortably. "Rumor has it that some kids escaped from a center. That they're top DRM priority."

"That so?"

"Story goes, one of them, a girl, is the long forgotten illegal of a certain member of Congress. With a simple DNA comparison, the entire system could be brought to its knees."

Blackwood laughed but glanced questioningly at Maggie. "If it were that easy, don't you think it'd be done by now? Regardless of all your rumors, we need a car. And be honest with yourself – you know if you don't give me one, I'll just steal one in the night. Choice is yours."

Lenkin exhaled. "I honestly don't have one. Some of our boys went on a run and will be back in the morning. You can have your car then."

"Guess we'll just make ourselves comfortable."

As soon as they left the tent, Blackwood disappeared, leaving the three companions on their own. Maggie pointed out a small clearing between the edge of the woods and the line of tents where they could make camp. Within minutes, they had a small fire going and food cooking.

"Thank God we're done with all that walking," Wick said. "I don't know about you guys, but I'm sick of it."

"I know. I don't think I could've taken another day of it." Maggie laughed. She felt surprisingly light as they sat near the safety of the encampment.

"Better be careful. Wouldn't want our faithful guide to hear you," Ryker said sarcastically.

"What's with the attitude?" It struck a nerve. His brooding had been wearing thin on Maggie since he attacked Blackwood. "He got us here, didn't he? Got us a new car."

"Did he? Where's that at? I wonder if he's even part of the Resistance or just another one of them like Wick. Seems everything you guys do is counterproductive to the movement." His tone was steady.

"You're ridiculous. If that were true, we wouldn't be here right now. The only counterproductive thing we've done is drag you along with us," Maggie said.

"Wick, I'd be careful if I were you. Look how quickly she turns on people she claims to care about."

"Stop," Wick said, but he wasn't looking at them. He stared out into the woods as a small amount of light danced off the fire onto the trees around them.

"What about you? You act like this is all my fault, like I wanted this to happen. As I recall, you came and broke me out. You let Luke and Jules come along." Ryker's eyes narrowed, and she knew she'd struck a nerve. "Exactly. This is as much your fault as it is mine. So why don't you stop with the attitude and actually offer something useful for a change!"

"Be quiet." Wick stood and walked away from the fire. Both Ryker and Maggie glanced at him, but immediately, their eyes met again.

"Offer something useful? Ok. How about going by car with an old man who needs drugs just to breathe, was that a bad idea? Or should we have allowed the Resistance to help us plan better?"

"That's not useful!" Maggie shouted.

"Shut it!" Wick hissed.

They both looked at him, their anger finding a new target, but Maggie felt anger turn to fear as she saw the look on his face. Something was wrong. They all froze. Waiting. Listening to the forest wall around them. Suddenly, Wick ran to the fire and started desperately throwing dirt on it, using his hands to quiet the flames. His panic banished any fear of burns. Maggie searched the wood line, looking for the cause of his concern, but she couldn't see anything.

"There are people out there," he whispered.

None of them moved. The camp hung behind them in eerie silence. She could only hear the wind blowing through the trees, a distant owl and animals in the brush, but then something strange carried through the air. A voice. It was difficult to determine from what direction it was coming. She looked at Ryker and was shocked to see him pull a knife from his pocket. She shook her head, but he looked away, his gaze resting back on the dark forest.

A woman's scream pierced the night air behind them. They all spun toward the camp as more screams rose above the silence, followed by blinding lights awakening the dark. No one moved even as they saw people running and madness taking over.

"Remos!" A single voice rang through the chaos.

"We have to get out of here," Maggie said, grabbing the backpack next to her.

"We should go on the offensive. Go get them." Ryker stood, his knife still in hand as he walked closer to the others.

"You want to go after Remos?" Maggie asked.

"You'll just get yourself captured or killed. We need to find Blackwood," Wick said, grabbing the second bag.

A young boy and girl came running toward them, and Maggie's heart stopped as adrenaline surged. The children were no more than six and eight.

"Remos," the girl breathed. Her eyes were wide with fear.

"Get close to the tent," Ryker instructed.

They all followed his lead, hiding just in the shadows of the nearest tent.

"You two take the kids and go hide in the woods. I'll deal with the Remos." Ryker tightened his grip on the knife.

"Don't be stupid. You'll just get yourself killed." She glanced at the mayhem and could see everyone panicking. People ran in every direction as Remos tackled them to the ground, using clubs and stun guns without prejudice.

She swallowed hard knowing their guide was somewhere in the middle of it. "I'll –"

"You should be on my side," Ryker said, stepping toward her. "Don't you want revenge for what they've done to us? For what they've done to our families?"

"Ryker—"

"You know I'm right. They made our families nothing. Treated our parents like they're less than human. Who knows what they've done to Luke and Jules. It's time we show them that we're not going to stand by and take it." His eyes looked wild in the moonlight, and Maggie was fearful of what he might do. The kids watched in silent awe.

"You kids should come with us." Wick peered around the tent, looking for any sign of intruders headed their way.

"I'm not going." Ryker shook his head.

She shouldered her pack and grabbed his arm. "We stay together, no matter what. That was the deal."

His eyes softened. "Maggie, I need to do this."

"No, you don't."

"We're wasting time, we need to move," Wick said.

Maggie's head spun. She couldn't leave her brother, but she knew to stay was suicide. She looked between the two, both pleading with her to follow them. Suddenly, the little boy started screaming.

Chapter Twenty

The noise echoed around them, bringing the chaos closer than it had been before. The girl grabbed the little boy and begged him to stop, to be quiet, but he only continued screaming. Maggie stared at the scene until her eyes fell on the dart sticking out of the boy's neck. It was exactly how Jules had described what happened to Luke. Right as this registered in her mind, a second dart hit the girl. A moment later, she fell to the ground screaming.

Wick picked up the little girl and pulled the dart from her neck. "Ryker, get the boy!"

He looked from the boy to his knife and begrudgingly shoved it away. He pulled out the dart as he lifted the small body up.

"Get them out of here. I'll find Blackwood." Maggie knew they'd try to stop her, but it had to be done. Without waiting for a response, she dashed from the shadows and ran toward the cries and glowing lights.

Their protests died in the air as gunfire and terror took over. She made her way toward the center of camp, knowing Blackwood would likely be with the camp leaders. People scattered in different directions as large men in all black burst into tent after tent.

When she finally reached the center tent, it appeared to be the only one untouched by the attack. The flaps hung still and no noise came forth. She ducked into the tent and slipped to the ground as she came to a sudden halt inside.

Four Remos stood around the center table with their flashlights searching at the papers spread across it. On the ground beside them lay several bodies, all of which were lifeless yet impossible to recognize in the dark. For a moment, Maggie simply stared, but she was startled back to her senses as one of the beams moved from the table to her face. She jumped to her feet as two Remos charged.

She ran through the crowd, suddenly feeling more a part of the group than she had before. She took a hard left, maneuvering between two tents arranged closely together. The backpack scraped against the tent walls, and she prayed it'd be difficult for the bulky men to follow. Just as she reached the end of the narrow opening, she was jerked backward. She looked back in terror as a Remo pawed the bag, trying to drag her body closer, though it was difficult for him to get leverage in such a tight space. Maggie tried to pull the sack from his grasp, but it was no use. Her feet slipped against the wet grass as he pulled her further and further back.

"Go around to the other side!" the Remo yelled.

Knowing she had to get out of the trap, she slid her arms from the straps and ran out of the alley. The Remo flew backward as his own momentum sent him to the ground. She followed the edge of the tent around, looking for a way back to the center of camp. Despite the danger, she refused to leave without Blackwood. Just as she was nearing her goal, she saw the shadow coming from where she had just been. Maggie ducked through a tent opening next to her and exhaled quietly when she saw that it was empty.

"Did you see her?" a Remo yelled.

"No, she didn't come this way. Probably into the woods."

"Let's go!"

Maggie waited a few seconds and then cautiously emerged. She stepped toward the brightly illuminated area, but stopped while still in the shadows. She scanned the crowds for Blackwood, but it was difficult to make out faces. Then, she saw him. He was just opposite her, leaning in the shadows of a tent across the main walkway of the campsite. He held up his hand, telling her to stay put. She nodded as he glanced back and forth, and then ran toward her. She was impressed by how fast he could move, and she realized he wasn't as old as she had thought.

He dodged around frantic people and Remos, but only feet from her, he was tackled to the ground. Two Remos pinned him down and tried to pull his arms behind his back. Blackwood fought like a rabid dog. He sunk his teeth into one of the Remos' hands, biting deeper and deeper until the man was forced to release his grip. Maggie grabbed a tent spike that was impaled in the ground in front of her and pulled up with all of her strength. Slowly, the thick piece of wood slipped from the ground, revealing it to be nearly a foot in length.

She ran toward the struggling men and struck one of the Remos in the head, sending him off Blackwood to the ground. Blackwood smashed his elbow into the other Remos' face over and over until the man fell on his back, motionless.

"What are you still doing here?" he growled, looking around for any signs of another attack.

"I'm here to get you."

He grunted. "Let's go."

He pushed her toward the tents and forest beyond. They ran as fast as they could and were only a few minutes into the woods when Blackwood grabbed her arm and jerked her to the ground. She looked at him and he held his finger to his lips. The screaming from the camp could still be heard, though it was muffled by the thick, silence of the forest. A branch snapped. Then another one. Though her heart raced, she held completely still.

Footsteps were coming up directly behind them, moving slowly and deliberately. They were searching. Maggie could feel someone standing above her, but she dared not move, keeping her eyes to the dirt below. Seconds dragged by, seeming to fill minute after minute. Finally, just as slowly as they had approached, the footsteps retreated. They lay frozen to the ground for several more minutes.

"Aren't you cool under pressure?" Blackwood eyed her as he stood up.

He led her further into the forest. It was impossible to see what was in front of them, making it difficult not to break every twig in their path. Things became even more challenging when they came to a steep hill that led, from what Maggie could tell, into nothingness.

"We're going to break our necks trying to get down there in the dark." She tried to make out the expression on his face, but it was no use. It was too black.

"My apologies, darling. I seem to have forgotten my flashlight."

"Listen—"

"Go slow, and you'll be fine."

Blackwood started down the incline, leaving her no choice but to follow. Maggie grabbed trees and downed logs – anything to try and keep her balance. The leaves were wet under her feet, making it impossible to stay upright. After falling twice, she kept one knee on the ground and slid slowly down. Water soaked through her jeans as she went, making her suddenly aware of the cold night air, but she felt more secure. Once at the bottom, Blackwood didn't slow. They continued for another half an hour until finding a thick cluster of trees.

"We'll stay here tonight and make our way to the contingency spot in the morning," Blackwood said. He squeezed through the narrow space between the trees until Maggie could no longer make out his shape.

She followed him, finding the space tight even for her, but was amazed to discover a small opening in the center. Blackwood was on the ground leaning against the trees for support and patted the open spot next to him. She sat down, and though they were uncomfortably close, she was relieved to no longer be moving blindly.

"What's a contingency point?" she asked.

He sighed. "Any time you have a sizable group of illegals living together, they're going be part of the Resistance in one way or another. Each of these groups establishes a safe location of sorts, a place where they can meet up if their camp is raided. It's a safety precaution, way to regroup." Blackwood laughed softly. "'Course you'd think more effort would be put into avoiding the raid in the first place."

"Will Wick know where that is?"

"They don't exactly publish a book filled with contingency locations." He put his collar up.

"We need to find them. They have two little kids with them." She sat upright, no longer wanting to rest.

"No one's finding anyone in these woods tonight. Consider that a blessing, darling. We'll make our way to the contingency tomorrow, and hopefully, we'll be able to pick up a car."

"I'm not—"

"If they really have kids from the camp with them, they'll be fine. Those kids will know where to go. They're trained to." He paused for a moment. "Let me ask you something. I know you're the important one. That much they told me. As it was put, do whatever you have to do to get that girl where she needs to be. Connecticut, if I'm not mistaken?"

She nodded. "That's right." He watched her as he spoke, and surprisingly, she didn't feel uncomfortable under his gaze.

"So, my question is, what makes you so important? Why does the Resistance suddenly care about some teenage runner? Or better yet, why have Remos been on my ass since I picked you up?"

Maggie was certain Ryker and Wick wouldn't want her telling him the truth, but somehow she knew she could trust him. He could be an ally if she let him. She took a deep breath. "My mother is Elizabeth Fullbrook."

Blackwood laughed. "It's been too long of a night for jokes, darling."

"It's the truth. She gave birth to me illegally, and her father covered it up by altering the records. We're going to make that information public and try to—"

"Swing the election." He rubbed the stubble on his chin but stopped as he leaned closer. "If she loses and the other guy follows through, the DRM could be shut down forever."

"Exactly."

"And you're ok with doing that to your mother?"

Maggie squared her shoulders to him. "She's no more my mother than I am her daughter." Bitterness hung on every word. "We're going to Connecticut to get pictures of her and my father together. Proof of their relationship."

He shook his head. "Pictures aren't going to work. There could be a million reasons why your parents are in a photo together, and none of them include breaking the law. If you really want people to care, let alone believe you, you'll need something a lot better than that."

"What do you suggest?" She wanted the case against Elizabeth to be airtight. They only had one chance at it.

"Well, Fullbrook lives in Connecticut. It seems kind of fortuitous that you're already going to be there, so why waste it? If I were you, I'd go to her house and get some of her DNA. Something to compare to yours. No one can argue against DNA, darling."

She laughed. "You want us to break into her house? That's insane. That can't even be possible."

"It'll be tough, that's for sure. And I'm not saying it wouldn't be awfully dangerous." Blackwood sat up straighter and grabbed her shoulders tightly. They stared at each other. "But you're a stronger weapon than you even know. You have the power to command the Resistance's help, assuming taking down the DRM is what's most important to you." Even in the darkness, she could see his jaw tighten as he released his grip and took the familiar blue box from his pocket. He stared at it and sighed. "But you should know, if that's not what's most important, be cautious about how much of that power you're willing to give to them."

Maggie watched as he put the box to his lips and inhaled. She wanted to talk more about the Resistance, but with Ryker no longer around, she felt her curiosity getting the better of her. "What is that?"

Blackwood shoved the box back into his pocket and leaned his head back against the tree. "You may be quite unique, darling, but we all have a past to deal with."

"But—"

"Leave it." The sadness in his voice stopped the next question from escaping her lips. He stared into the night and Maggie wondered what had happened to him. She shuddered

"You won't tell anyone about what we're doing, will you?" She had to ask.

"No. But I hope you realize that this type of thing – who you are and what you're trying to do – people kill over things like this. I won't tell anyone, but be very careful about who you choose to tell. Blind faith isn't a luxury you have any more."

Chapter Twenty-one

The morning light broke through the treetops, but that wasn't what woke Maggie. She and Blackwood were already up and on the move. Even before dawn was on the horizon, the pair decided to get going. They knew they couldn't wait. Compared to their silence, the sounds of their feet against the forest floor and the rhythmic beat of Blackwood's walking stick as he moved, both seemed louder than they possibly could've been. Still, Maggie's thoughts were busy replaying her conversation with Blackwood. It was burned in her mind and she could only guess it was because he was right. They needed to adjust their plan and she needed to get Wick and Ryker on board.

After several hours, they stopped abruptly. Blackwood stared out ahead of them, every muscle tense.

"What is it?" Maggie whispered. She could see a small road 50 yards in front of them. From the looks of it, a highway had been carved directly into the landscape, leaving a large embankment on either side.

"Once we get to the other side, it's only another hour."

"I'm not exactly excited about the idea of running across an expressway."

Blackwood looked at her and had a hint of a smile on his face. "I'll see what I can do."

They continued through the woods, using the highway as a guide. Maggie kept her eyes to the road. Even though it was barely noticeable through the thicket, she scanned for any sign of patrolling Remos. She saw it before Blackwood. A small walkway that extended over the highway.

"Look over there."

Blackwood stopped and stared for a moment. He nodded. "That'll do."

A branch snapped behind them and they both spun around. Maggie couldn't see anything but was certain what she'd heard. It had to be footsteps. It was too loud and distinct to be anything else. Blackwood was frozen in place. Every muscle was tense and on high alert. Another branch snapped, but this time, to their right. They both turned right as the shadow emerged. Blackwood swung his heavy walking stick, but the person ducked and brought his fist around to counterattack. Before the punch could land, Wick burst from the woods and knocked the attacker to the ground.

"Get off me!"

"Ryker?" Maggie could barely believe what she was seeing.

Wick squirmed off her brother and stood up, smiling. "I told him not to surprise you."

Maggie threw her arms around him. "I was so worried. Are you both all right?"

"*You* were worried?" Ryker asked as he stood up. "The last time we saw you, you were running toward Remos. What's wrong with you? You're the one person they can't get, and you go do something that stupid?"

She released Wick and looked at her brother. "Someone had to find him." She nodded at Blackwood. "And you both had your hands full with the kids."

"No one had to find him. We could've all just met at the contingency point," Ryker snapped. He stepped closer to her and his eyes grew dark. "This is what I meant about being counterproductive."

"Not that again. What was all that business with the knife then? There were loads of Remos, what do you really think you would've accomplished?"

"You wanted a plan. That was a plan."

"So is what I did. The only difference is, mine actually worked."

Ryker took another step forward, but before he could speak, Blackwood interrupted. "How'd you get here?"

Wick whistled, then the boy and girl appeared from the woods. "They know exactly where the contingency spot is." The girl handed him the familiar backpack.

Maggie shifted on her feet. "Just so you guys know, I lost the other bag."

"How'd that happen?" Ryker's voice was harsh.

"It doesn't matter. We need to keep moving," Blackwood said, pushing past them and continuing toward the bridge.

Wick half smiled at Maggie as they followed. They walked in silence until coming to a halt just short of the bridge's entrance, though they were careful to stay within the tree line.

"That's going to be dangerous." Ryker looked from the bridge to the surrounding forest.

Maggie followed his gaze. "Why?"

"If there are any Remos around, this is where they'll trap us. If they know where the contingency spot is, they'll already be waiting."

It dawned on her, yet again, what a good Remo her brother would make. She wondered how he would feel if she told him.

"We'll send the kids first," Ryker said.

"Are you kidding?" She couldn't believe what she'd heard. "I'll go first."

The kids watched the conversation closely but didn't move.

"If they're already waiting, they won't want the kids. They'll want us. If we send them first, they'll have a chance to get away in case we're captured."

Maggie couldn't help but smile.

"How do you know they even know about you?" the girl asked. "They'll be rounding up anyone they can find from the camp." It was obvious she was old for her age.

"They won't risk exposing themselves for kids," Wick said.

"The boy's got a good point. It's been less than twelve hours since the raid and they're still looking for a big score. Wait a few more hours and they'll be happy as pie with just you rugrats." Blackwood scratched his grey stubble as he stared at the bridge. "Still. You never know."

Ryker knelt down in front of the kids, bringing him to their level. "Walk out there as calmly as you can. Do not run across the bridge. If you don't see anything on the other side, go twenty feet and cut into the woods. Cut to the left."

"You sound like a Remo," the girl mumbled as she grabbed the boy's hand.

Ryker's jaw tightened but he didn't respond. They stood still, all eyes watching as the two children crossed the bridge. Maggie could see the girl's grip tighten as her brother tried to pull them faster across the walkway, however, she kept the pace steady.

"Why did you tell them to go left?" Wick asked.

"People's natural instinct is to turn right, so it's easier to anticipate."

Blackwood was the only one of them looking away

from the bridge. He stared at Ryker, watching his every move, and Maggie could see there was distrust buried in his eyes. After a couple of agonizing minutes, they were over. She sighed in relief.

"Maggie, you go next," Wick said.

She laughed. "No."

"They'll wait for us, it'll be safer if you go now." He tried to nudge her out onto the path.

"We do not have time for this. No one grabbed the kids, there isn't anyone out there." Ryker pushed by them and marched across the walkway without the faintest hesitation.

"That little girl's right. Your brother does give off a certain air of Remo," Blackwood mused as he too walked passed.

Maggie was frozen to the ground in disbelief at what her brother had just done. Wick grabbed her hand and pulled her forward. "Come on."

He gave a weak smile as they crossed the bridge. All she could think about was Ryker. What was happening to him? Blackwood glanced back at them and raised an eyebrow as he saw their intertwined hands. As if on cue, Wick squeezed her hand, simultaneously making her heart flutter and her face burn red. She pulled her hand free, rather ungracefully, and shoved it into her pocket, which only made Blackwood chuckle as he turned around.

Maggie didn't dare look at Wick, knowing he would

only distract her. She needed to focus on her brother. Something was happening to him. He wasn't the same person she'd grown up with at Jessup. Dread grew in the pit of her stomach as she wondered how to stifle his growing rage and indifference. And more terrifyingly, she questioned whether it was even possible.

Chapter Twenty-two

Only three hours after crossing the bridge, they had a car and were back on the road. It was amazing how quick the Resistance was willing to help, even though Blackwood refused to give them any information about their mission. The SUV they were given was old and seemed like it would barely run, but it had plenty of space. More importantly, it was the first time in days they weren't traveling on foot, and as a result, the entire group was in a considerably better mood.

"You must have a plan on how we're going to get across the border," Ryker said suddenly. They'd been riding in silence for an hour, enjoying the relative peace of the drive.

"Nope. They just call me a border specialist to confuse folks." Blackwood's grip tightened on the steering wheel, despite the levity in his voice. Maggie was sitting behind the passenger seat where Ryker had insisted on helping to navigate.

"Ryker, I know this might be hard to believe, but Blackwood is known as one of the best when it comes to crossing borders undetected." Wick stretched his arms out, clearly enjoying the extra room of the backseat.

"Yeah, things have been going great so far."

"You're welcome to get out and walk," Blackwood growled.

"So, what is the plan?" Maggie asked, ignoring both of their comments.

"Quite simple, darling. We walk across."

"That's your master plan?" Ryker sat forward, looking from Blackwood back to Maggie. "I thought you hated walking."

"It worked leaving Michigan, didn't it?" Wick said.

"He said it himself that getting into New York is one of the hardest things to do."

Blackwood pulled the blue box from his pocket, put it to his lips, and took a long inhale. He coughed softly as he stretched his neck back and forth, causing the joints to crack loudly. Once again, Maggie's curiosity peaked. She could tell it was an unpleasant experience and wondered why he continued to do it. "That's exactly why we're walking."

"What is that thing?" Ryker demanded.

"None of your damn business." Blackwood turned on the radio to drown out any further discussion.

An hour later, they pulled back off the expressway. The road soon gave way to nothing more than a dirt path, which looked barely used. Maggie felt on edge, wanting to get the crossing over with, and as they drove further through the back roads, her anxiety grew. Finally, the truck stopped.

"Don't," Blackwood said. Maggie's hand was on the door handle, and though he was looking forward, he'd somehow seen. "Wait here."

He left the car, quietly closing his door behind him. He stepped just inside the tree line and, immediately, two other bodies appeared.

"Did you see that?" she asked.

"Yeah." Wick moved closer to her as he strained for a better view.

"They're not Remos," Ryker said.

Even though it was difficult to make out their features, she could see he was right. It was a man and woman, and rather than attack Blackwood, they were yelling at him. After several minutes, they finally stepped clear of the forest's camouflage. The man and woman looked similar to one another, both with dark red hair and pale skin. They looked to be in their mid-twenties, though their faces were contorted with anger, making it difficult to be certain. The woman grabbed Blackwood's arm and stopped him from walking. He turned in a flash and Maggie thought their argument might actually turn physical.

She opened her door. "We don't have time for this."

Ryker jumped from the SUV and shoved her door

closed. "I'll deal with it." He slammed his own door before she could protest.

"I'm going to kill him one of these days," Maggie said, but before she could follow him, the woman grabbed Ryker and pulled him hurriedly into the woods. Blackwood and the man followed as both of their faces strained with alarm. "What are they doing?"

Wick shoved Maggie to the floor. It happened so unexpectedly, she had no time to brace herself and slammed painfully to the bottom. "Get under the seat!" he hissed as he threw himself over the front seat and behind the steering wheel. There was complete panic in his voice. "Remos just pulled up behind us."

+ + +

Her heart raced as she struggled to cram herself into the small space below the seat. Garbage and sharp pieces of metal lay as obstacles along her path, but she ignored the pain of them poking into her body. Flat on her stomach, she was just able to fit, though the pressure on her ribs made it difficult to breathe.

"Sir, can you please explain what you are doing here?" The voice was sharp and menacing – it was a Remo. She held her breath, fearful he would hear her.

"I'm trying to find the expressway, but admittedly, I'm completely lost," Wick said calmly. "I'm driving from Pennsylvania to New York, and I've had one hell of a trip."

"Sir, you're several miles from the expressway. How did you end up on this road?" Suspicion hung on every word.

"My car broke down and was towed to this small town. After a few days of them not being able to fix it, I rented this SUV, but getting from the rental office to the expressway has been impossible."

The cramped position caused her heartbeat to pulse in her ears, and along with the Remos' occasional mumbling, it made it difficult for her to hear. She prayed Ryker was safely hidden in the woods with the others.

"You will follow us to the border, where you will be vetted. If you deviate from our lead, we will consider you a criminal and you will be placed under arrest. Do you understand?"

"Yes. I'm honestly happy for you to lead me there. Who knows, I might've been trapped in these woods for hours. They're very confusing."

Silence took the small space and Maggie strained to hear anything that might indicate what was happening.

"Are you ok?" Wick asked. She didn't answer. She wasn't certain he was speaking to her. "Maggie?"

"I'm ok," she said softly. Her lungs were too constricted to project her voice properly. She could feel the SUV begin to move slowly.

"I'm…I'm so sorry."

"What do you mean?" They hit a bump as they

picked up speed, slamming her body painfully up and down. She exhaled loudly as she tried to maneuver out of the space.

"Don't come out," he said quickly." They're in front of us, and if they think someone else is in here, they'll tear this thing apart."

She begrudgingly slipped back into position. Each turn of the wheel sent painful vibrations through her body. Her hips continued to smash against some sort of sharp metal, and each time, she had to bite her lip.

"We're going across the border. Both of us."

"We're going to be arrested," she said as panic set in.

"No, we're not. We're going to get through this." Wick's voice was calm, but she knew he had to be as nervous as she was.

"What about Ryker and Blackwood? If we're arrested, those two will kill each other on their own. Wick, we can't go across that border."

"We don't have a choice." He took a deep breath. "I can see it. We're almost there."

"Wick—"

"No matter what happens, no matter what you hear, do not come out of there. Do you understand?"

She didn't answer. Sweat poured down her face as she tried to calm her breathing, but panic was taking over.

"Maggie! Tell me you understand."

"I understand," she said finally.

The SUV hit a hard bump and slammed her hips into the metal once again. She felt as if they pierced through her pants and cut into her skin. Maggie grinded her teeth to keep any noise from escaping. She had to be quiet and Wick had to focus. She could feel them slowing, and as they pulled to a stop, the throbbing in her hips eased.

"Good Afternoon," Wick said cheerfully. This was it. She held her breath, listening closely to every word.

"According to my colleagues, you were on a back road approaching the border. Why?" The voice was harsh and direct.

"I was lost. I'd been looking for the expressway for hours." It amazed her how steady his voice remained.

"You realize I can look at traffic cameras set up over the last hundred miles of highway to determine if you're lying?"

Fear pierced her heart.

"Yes, of course, but I assume you'd like to scan my ID?"

The Remo paused before answering. "Why would you assume that?"

Wick laughed. "It's procedure, isn't it?"

Maggie didn't understand why he was asking to be scanned. Why wasn't he trying to talk his way around that? She willed him to shut up.

"It's at the Officer's discretion, actually. As is determining the need for further investigation."

"Further investigation?"

"Sir, please step out of the vehicle."

For a moment, Wick didn't move. Maggie could see his feet just across from her face, but then the door opened, and he slipped out of the SUV. Her heart raced as light intruded toward her. She forced her body not to move, afraid that any sound would give her away.

"Your hand please." The Remos' voice seemed closer.

"A blood sample? Really?" Wick asked.

Her mind searched for a solution. Running wouldn't help. It was only a matter of time, seconds really, before the test results would appear and all would be lost. They would arrest him and then tear the car apart. She'd be discovered. As her heart raced faster, it became difficult to breathe. Her body was so constricted, her lungs physically could not expand wide enough to get the oxygen her racing heart required. She began to feel lightheaded.

"Let's see who you really are," the Remo said as the familiar beep sounded. "Wick, is it?"

That was it. Their cover was blown.

The Remo started laughing. "Why didn't you tell me your brother was an Officer?"

Chapter Twenty-three

Maggie was certain she'd misheard him. Her pulse was loud in her ears and she was dizzy from not being able to breathe. It was impossible she had heard correctly.

"He was killed in the line of duty. It's kind of hard to talk about," Wick said.

"I'm sorry. How long ago did it happen?"

"A few years. It feels like just last week though." There was real grief in his voice. This wasn't a made-up story.

"It always does. Do you mind me asking how he died?" The Remos' tone had taken a 180-degree turn, going from harsh and suspicious to empathetic in a second.

"He was killed during a raid on a Resistance camp." His voice broke, but he coughed in an attempt to cover it up. "It's ok though, his partner got the guy who did it."

"They arrested him?"

"Nope."

The Remo laughed darkly. Maggie's stomach turned.

Her panic had not subsided, though it was hampered by confusion and fear. Was Wick lying to the Remo or had he been lying to her?

"In the future, if you are caught in a situation like this, you really should be upfront about your brother. It would make things a lot easier."

"I'll keep that in mind, though hopefully I don't need to explain myself anytime soon," Wick said as he got back in the SUV. He slammed the door shut, sending painful vibrations through Maggie's body.

The SUV started moving, happening so unexpectedly that she had no time to brace herself. There was only silence and she feared what was happening. Was Wick driving her to be arrested? Had he given her up? Sweat dripped down her forehead and into her eyes, but she was too cramped to wipe it away.

"You can come out. I can't believe it, but we actually made it through," he said suddenly.

She didn't move.

"Are you all right down there?" There was concern in his voice. "I can't stop yet, they'll be watching."

"I'm fine." Her voice was so soft that she wondered if he could even hear it. As carefully as possible, Maggie maneuvered out of the tight space. As she slipped out, the metal dragged along her hips, cutting deeper into her skin, but she barely noticed

"Stay in the footwell for now," Wick said, glancing quickly from the road to her.

She leaned against the right passenger door and took several deep breaths as she watched him drive. Only now that her lungs could fully expand did she realize just how constricted they had been. Each breath helped to focus her mind and fight away the dizziness.

"Who are you?" Maggie stared at him, wanting to watch every move he made. She needed to know more before she could determine if he could be trusted.

Wick glanced at her and smiled. "What do you mean?"

"Don't lie to me. I heard what you said to him." She struggled to keep her voice steady as fear turned to anger.

"I was lying to him to get us through the border." His jaw tightened.

"He did a blood test. Those don't lie."

"This coming from the girl whose blood is the biggest lie of all?" he said sharply.

"You said yourself that it's almost impossible to change blood results. Tell me the truth."

"What do you want me to say?"

"Tell me how your brother is a Remo!" she yelled as her fist slammed down on the backseat. "How is it possible for you to be an orphan of the Resistance while he's trying to destroy it?"

He opened his mouth but then closed it. He stared forward intensely, but even from where she sat, Maggie could see she'd struck a nerve. "You don't understand," he said finally.

"Help me to understand. I mean, how can I trust anything you've said? Are you really trying to help us?" All her fear and panic over the last hour came rushing out in pure rage.

He looked at her, startled. "How can you even ask me that? I've been trekking through the woods for days, putting up with your brother, who apparently knows everything about the Resistance. I saved you from those Remos back in Michigan, and I stopped you when you were about to commit suicide at the DRM. I've even stuck around to make sure Blackwood and the other guides hold up their end. So don't tell me I'm not helping."

"That doesn't change the fact you've been lying to us. Why?"

Wick took a deep breath. "Do you remember that story Ryker told you when we were with Morrigan?"

She thought for a moment. "About the men sent undercover with the DRM?"

"One of those men was my brother."

"You said those men were discovered and killed, along with their families."

"My brother was discovered by the DRM. They took his blood and hunted down every family member they could find. I told you my parents were killed when I was nine. That's true. They didn't even try to arrest them. It was murder. My aunts, uncles, cousins – everyone was killed."

"Except for you?" Her anger subsided with each passing second. His shoulders tightened and his knuckles turned white against the steering wheel as he nodded.

"We were in a small camp in an abandoned wheel factory when they attacked. People ran in every direction. We headed for the back halls that led to the boiler room; from there you could get to the sewers. They shot my mom before we made it. Dad wouldn't let me stop for her. He dragged me to the boiler room as I fought to go back, and right as he lifted the sewer grate, Remos appeared. The last thing I remember is my Dad yelling for me to jump into the sewer, and right as I did, they shot him."

"Oh my God." The scene played clearly in her mind and made her stomach turn.

"They came after me, calling my name specifically. But I lost them in the sewer when I finally found a pipe too small for any of them to get down. Eventually, they were forced to leave. Afterward, I found the Resistance, and they were pretty surprised to see me alive." He laughed hollowly. "That's when I found out that my brother had been discovered, and this was the DRM's retaliation."

"And your brother?"

"They killed him. Left him for us to find."

For a moment, she didn't answer as she processed

everything. "That doesn't make sense."

His face hardened.

"Why would your brother still be labeled a Remo in the system if he wasn't really one?" She tried to choose her words carefully, seeing the anger in his eyes.

"They had no choice. If they labeled him a spy, one who was already in their custody, they'd have to explain how he died. But by leaving him a Remo, they could kill him, dump his body, and then blame the Resistance. I did some digging, and according to his personal file, he was killed in action by Resistance forces. It's ridiculous." Wick cracked his neck from side to side.

"Why isn't your file still flagged?"

"The flag automatically dropped from my file last year when I turned eighteen. They didn't have a justifiable reason to keep it anymore."

"I thought you were underage?"

He glanced at her with a smirk. "My file says I'm nineteen, but I'm really sixteen. After I was able to hack into my brother's personal file, I changed my information. They had my birthday, an old picture, everything. I upped it by three years, knowing that was all I'd be able to get away with, without drawing too much attention."

"So all this time you knew if they demanded a blood test, you'd get through without a problem?" Her anger steadily came back.

He hesitated but then nodded. "Yes."

"Why didn't you tell us?" she demanded.

"Very few people know about my family history. It's not exactly easy to explain how your brother is listed in the system as a decorated Remo. It's even more difficult when I have someone like Ryker or Blackwood monitoring everything I say and do."

Guilt churned in her stomach. She'd been so focused on getting the truth, she'd forgotten momentarily about her brother. Anything could have happened to him. "We have to find the others."

Chapter Twenty-four

Half an hour after they made it through the border, Maggie finally moved from the floor to the passenger seat. Once sitting upright, she investigated the damage from the uncomfortable crossing. As she'd suspected, her jeans were torn right above her hips, through which she could see several cuts.

"Are you ok?" Wick's eyes darted from her to the road.

"Yeah, I'm fine." She pulled her shirt down to cover the blood.

They had driven in silence since their conversation had come to an abrupt end. Maggie was still trying to process everything Wick had said. She knew his parents had been killed, but she never would've guessed his entire family. Having Ryker, and knowing she had an uncle out there, made all the difference in the world. She wanted to grab his hand to show him some support, but she resisted. He still seemed offended by her inquest, and she continued to remind herself that she had a right to be angry as well.

"We'll get off at the next exit and circle around," he said suddenly.

She nodded. "Do you think they've made it over the border?"

"Probably. So long as they weren't stopped."

"Don't even think like that." Her hands squeezed together as she stared out the window.

Wick glanced at her. "Sorry. I'm sure he's fine."

They pulled off the expressway, taking a small, one-lane road back into the woods. Maggie scanned the trees as they drove, despite knowing they had a couple miles before they were in the right area. Finally, the SUV pulled to a stop. Though they were exactly across the border from where they had been separated, there was no road. She opened the door, but he grabbed her arm, preventing her from getting out.

"What are you doing?" he asked.

"I'm going to look for them." Her eyes narrowed as she pulled her arm free.

"If Remos stopped them, they'll be here waiting for us. You should stay in the car, just in case."

Maggie laughed. "If they find you over here again, it won't matter what ace your blood holds."

She got out of the SUV and shut the door. The stress of not knowing if Ryker was ok was pushing her to her breaking point, and yet there was a certain calm in having him gone. His anger was no longer hanging heavily around them, and she felt guilty for experiencing a sense of relief. She scanned the tree line and cautiously made her way into the forest. Wick came jogging up behind her, but she didn't look back. It was late in the day, and though it was still light outside, shadows cut through the trees.

"Do you see anything?" She tried to keep her voice quiet, just in case they weren't among friends.

"No." He looked at his watch. "They should've been able to cover this distance without a problem."

Maggie took another step forward but then stopped. She knew wandering around the woods was dangerous, especially this close to the border. But she also knew she wouldn't leave without doing everything in her power to find her brother. She glanced at Wick, making sure his eyes were elsewhere, and took a deep breath.

"Ryker!" she screamed. Her voice echoed through the woods.

Wick's hand clamped down hard over her mouth. "Are you crazy?"

She tried to pull free, but he stood behind her with one hand over her mouth and the other wrapped around her arms. His body felt warm against hers, but she didn't like being restricted in such a way. They struggled against one another until a branch snapped in the distance. Both of them froze, straining to hear and see from where it had come.

"Do not scream," Wick whispered as he released her.

She was too focused on the noise to be mad. Her head swiveled around and she could only see shadows and trees.

"Do you see anything?" she whispered.

"No. We should get back to the car."

Maggie nodded. Though neither would say it out loud, they both knew that if the worst should happen, they needed to be prepared to make a quick departure. They resumed their positions in the car in silence, both still watching the surrounding trees for any hint of movement. After several minutes passed without any sign of intruders, Maggie looked at Wick.

"Can I ask you something?"

He glanced back, looking uncertain if he wanted to answer. "Of course."

"What were those darts the kids were shot with?" They both spoke in hushed tones, worried they might somehow be heard from the woods.

He looked back out the window. "Shriekers. A recent addition to the Remo arsenal. They just came around a couple years ago. They make it possible for Remos to incapacitate and locate people easily. The darts are filled with a drug. When it hits a person, it freezes up their muscles, causing them to seize. It's impossible to run. Imagine every muscle in your body twisting and cramping all at once. The pain is unbearable, and that's what causes the screaming. As you can see, it's very effective."

"They're awful. Those screams..." She shook her head, trying to push the memories away.

"And that's still not the worst thing Remos are capable of." Wick's brow crinkled and she knew what he was thinking about. Noticing her look, he quickly added, "Like I said, I'm sure Ryker's fine."

Maggie half smiled, and her eyes shifted back to the darkening woods around them. "I might be overreacting, but he seems to have, I don't know, when he talks to me...I think something's wrong."

"Siblings fight, it's no big deal." He twirled the single car key between his fingers, gliding it from one to the next.

"This isn't just fighting. Every time I say anything, suggest anything, he has so much anger."

"A lot has happened over the last few days. I'm sure it's just getting to him."

Maggie looked at him and watched his methodic movement of the key. After several seconds, she grabbed his hand, forcing him to stop and look at her. "Then why is all of his anger directed at me? I can see his...hate."

Wick opened his mouth but then shut it as he looked away. "He doesn't hate you."

"You know something." Suspicion flared in her chest. "Did he say something to you?"

"No. Maybe we should move further down," he said dismissively as he continued to twirl the key back and forth.

She snatched it from his hand and his eyes blazed as they shot to hers. "Tell me what you know."

They stared at one another for several seconds before Wick finally sighed. "There are some things that are better not to know."

"If you want this back, you'll tell me."

He smirked. "Pretty sure I could take it if I wanted to."

"Try me." Her voice was stone.

Wick rubbed his face. He glanced at the trees, which were still and silent, and then back to Maggie. "He doesn't hate you, it's just, I think he's having trouble coming to terms with some of the things the Resistance told him."

"What things?" She had spent so much time trying to get on the road, she had no idea what Ryker had learned from them.

"He wanted to know why the DRM chose him and his family for your cover. He thought there was some connection or something, but the Resistance told him it was because they were nobodies. They could disappear and be given new identities, new kids, and no one would notice or care. They were worthless."

"Why would they tell him that?"

"Because it's true."

"They are not worthless." Her voice rose sharply in the small space.

"Shh." Wick held his hands up while looking once again to the darkness. "Of course they're not, not really, but from the DRM's point of view, no one would care. It's not just them, but anyone that's been arrested under the Reproduction Act. They don't care about any of them. The reason Ryker and his mother were chosen is simple – they probably fit the closest description of what was needed."

"So, he's mad at me because of that?"

Wick's jaw tightened and he shook his head. "No. The Resistance also told him that if his parents hadn't been pulled into this, then they'd likely still be alive. They told him they were murdered because of you."

Chapter Twenty-five

Maggie stared at him, letting the words slowly wash over her. She couldn't understand what she had just heard. "Because of me?"

Wick nodded.

"That doesn't make any sense." She shook her head.

"We know the DRM wants to cover up who your real mom is, and they did so by manipulating the database. As an infant, they probably kept you a secret at the center until you were three, and then they realized they needed a cover for you to officially enter the system. The only way that would be possible is if you were attached to a man or woman who was arrested, or at least, in the system. That was Henry, but the system would still want to know what happened to your mom. Don't you remember what his parents' records said?"

She thought hard. "His father was killed assaulting a Remo, and his mother..." She trailed off as she remembered the words.

"Died in childbirth." He nodded. "The only problem with that is, she died during childbirth four years after her only biological child was born. And you heard Silvia back in Lansing. She said Ryker's father was alive when he was taken into custody."

"They killed them to make my story more convincing." Maggie's voice was barely audible. Her stomach turned and she feared she might be sick. "Ryker's right. I am the reason they were killed."

Wick grabbed her hand. "No, you're not. It's possible they just said that in the file. It's entirely possible they both died in custody, and that's why they were chosen."

"What do you think is more likely? That they waited around for a dead couple to appear, or that they took matters into their own hands?" She tried to pull her hand away, but he held it firmly.

"Either way, it doesn't matter. You didn't come up with this plan. You were as much a victim of it as he was," he said softly.

She looked at him and saw determination in his eyes. She nodded halfheartedly. Something moved through the shadows just beyond him and caught her eye.

"Someone's out there," Maggie breathed.

Wick immediately turned to follow her gaze. They sat in tense silence as they both watched the shadow move.

She could plainly see that it was a person, and by the looks of it, a man. "It's Ryker."

"It's too dark to tell."

She shook her head. "It's him."

She opened her door and quickly jumped out to avoid Wick's hand that tried to grab her. She walked around the SUV, heading toward the shadow with unwavering confidence. He was right. She couldn't make out the person's features, but she was certain it was Ryker. She just knew it. Wick ran up beside her and tried to slow her down.

"Are you crazy? It could be Remos!" he hissed.

"If it was, we'd be arrested by now." She barely glanced at him as she continued.

"Look what a quick study someone is." Blackwood's voice rang out in the still air directly from their left.

They both looked as he stepped out of the shadows, followed immediately by the woman they'd seen earlier. Maggie glanced back toward the direction she'd been heading right as the man and Ryker stepped into sight.

"Thank God, you're all right." Ryker smiled as he walked toward them.

Maggie ran and hugged him, all thoughts of her conversation with Wick momentarily forgotten.

"You were on the other side of the road?" Wick looked back toward the state line, where they had been monitoring.

"We circled around, trying to get a look inside the truck. Could've been a bunch of Remos in there waiting for us." Blackwood rubbed his neck.

"How'd you make it across the border?" the woman asked.

Maggie looked from the woman to Blackwood. "Who're they?"

Before he could answer, she stepped in front of Maggie. "Your new guides. I'm Kalix." She pointed at the man. "And this is my brother, Elrick. We'll be taking it from here."

Maggie had been right. They looked to be in their mid-twenties, though the way they held themselves told her they'd experienced a lot in that time.

"We should've taken over from the other side, but someone insisted on coming along." Elrick glanced at Blackwood.

"I wanted to make sure you found them. Sue me."

"It doesn't matter." Kalix's tone was sharp and she watched Maggie and Wick with the intensity of a predator. "How did you make it across?"

"Why do you care? We're here," Wick said.

"Because what you just did is impossible. How did you do it?" Elrick took a step closer to them.

Maggie glanced from their new guides to Ryker and found the same suspicious look on his face. Wick squared his shoulders to them and she realized he was preparing for a fight.

"Wick talked his way across," she said. Although she was mad he had lied, she understood why he did. She wasn't sure they would. "I hid under the backseat. They believed him and let us go."

"That's not possible."

"It's what happened," Wick said.

Elrick took a step forward as did Kalix. Blackwood moved closer to Maggie, but rather than feeling comforted, she felt even more surrounded.

"There's no way Remos would find you that close to the border on a back road and not scan your ID. Let alone not test your blood. So the question is, what did it tell them that they just let you go right on through?" Kalix asked.

Wick's jaw tightened. For a moment, no one moved, but then, as if on cue, Elrick and Kalix lunged and tackled him to the ground. He managed to push Elrick off, but Kalix twisted his arm back, forcing him to halt his movement. Elrick pulled a small device with a menacing point from his pocket. Maggie ran forward and snatched it from his hand.

"Give that to me," he shouted.

"Let him up." Maggie's voice was firm, and her grip was tight.

"We're testing his blood whether you like it or not." Elrick advanced toward her and her hand shot to the knife on her belt. Before she could pull it free, arms closed around hers and pinned them to her sides. Maggie fought against the human constraints, pausing only when she realized it was her brother who was responsible. His betrayal fueled the anger in her chest and made her fight even harder.

Elrick seized the device from her hand and immediately knelt beside Wick. He struggled against Kalix's weight, but it was obvious every movement sent pain through his arm, straining it nearly to the breaking point.

"Ryker, don't let them do this!" Maggie shouted.

"We need to know." His voice was steady and empty.

The device gave a faint beep and the sharp prong was removed from Wick's skin. They waited in pained silence for the results.

"He's a Remo," Elrick said.

Without hesitating, Kalix pulled a knife from her boot and put it against Wick's throat.

"Wait! He's not a Remo!" Maggie elbowed her brother's chest even as she felt his grip already loosening. He grunted but gave enough slack that she slipped from his arms.

"It says here his brother was. He must be one too," Elrick said.

Maggie took a step forward, but Kalix tightened the knife against his throat. She feared moving any closer would result in his death. "First off, we're not all like our siblings." She couldn't help but throw Ryker a disgusted look. "Second, his brother was working undercover for the Resistance. He was only pretending to be a spy. Wick, tell them!"

"I'm not explaining myself to anyone," he strained

through clenched teeth.

Maggie exhaled in exasperation. "Blackwood, you know he's not a Remo."

The veteran stared at the scene, and for a moment, he didn't say a word. Finally, he shook his head. "Nah, this boy's no Remo. If he were, we'd have been arrested days ago. Hell, we wouldn't have made it out of Michigan."

Elrick and Kalix exchanged looks. "Maybe he's waiting until he can get more of us. Take down a larger part of the Resistance."

"This is the strongest weapon the Resistance has, right here. Let him up."

"What weapon?" Elrick asked.

"I said, let him up." Blackwood's voice grew darker.

No one moved, but then Kalix stood and finally released Wick. He pulled himself to a kneeling position but didn't get to his feet. His breathing was labored and it was only then that Maggie realized the pressure Kalix had been putting on his body.

"So, what weapon are you talking about?" Kalix asked, moving closer to Blackwood.

He laughed. "Why don't you just focus on getting these kids where they need to be, huh?"

Elrick nodded. "Yeah, all right. Probably time for you to be moving along anyway."

Blackwood grumbled something obscene to himself and stared at the pair of guides. Finally, he nodded and looked at Maggie. "Take care, darling."

"Wait." She grabbed his arm.

"What? I told you I'd get you here, and I did." His voice had the same edge to it as always.

She nodded. "Right. Well, thanks."

As she turned away, he grabbed her shoulder and pulled her close, taking her by surprise and causing her to stumble toward him. "You listen here, darling. These two will take you where you need to go, but don't for a second trust them. Or anyone. The DRM has just as many spies as we do, and just like ours, they'll be ruthless to the end. And above all else, don't tell anyone what you're after, or where you're going."

"Why don't you just take us the rest of the way?"

"Can't take on the DRM and the Resistance, kid. Don't worry." He glanced at their new guides and stealthily slipped a small bit of paper in her hand. "Just keep your eyes sharp, and if you ever need anything, call that number."

Maggie didn't dare look down. She gave him a tight hug, knowing she'd likely never see him again, but after only a second, he pulled away and strode into the darkness.

"We need to get out of here," Kalix said. "They drive this border constantly. It's amazing you two weren't already picked up."

"Of course, this still seemed like a great place to interrogate me," Wick mumbled as he stood up.

"Kalix's right. Grab anything you need from the

SUV." Elrick watched him as he moved.

"We're going to walk? We don't have time for that." Maggie glanced from Wick to Ryker. "We've already lost too many days."

"Listen, that SUV has been tagged. There's no way we can cross in it again, not even with pure blood over there. So get your things, we're leaving now." Kalix walked into the woods without a second glance. Ryker looked at Maggie, but then silently followed.

"They'll have a car further down. Remember, they were expecting us," Wick whispered as he moved past her to the SUV. He pulled their one remaining pack out, positioned it squarely on his shoulders, and then grabbed her hand as they followed the others into the darkness.

As much as she hated to admit it, his hand was a welcome comfort, and it made her almost smile knowing it meant the same to him. Her brother had betrayed her, and after learning what she had from Wick, it felt like it wasn't the first time. She hated him for that. She hated that Blackwood had left, and not only did she not trust their new guides, she worried about what they were capable of. There had been no hesitation in Kalix's eyes when it came to killing Wick. Still, she couldn't help but think of what Blackwood had said – you can't fight the DRM and the Resistance. She took a deep breath and hoped she wouldn't have to.

Chapter Twenty-six

Wick had been right. An SUV was waiting for them less than an hour's walk from where they had met. It was much newer than their previous vehicle, and it felt like something Remos would drive. Black, with dark tinted windows, black leather interior, and a top-of-the-line navigation system. Still, it was an uncomfortable ride. Maggie was stuck in the middle of the back seat, sitting square between Wick and Ryker, and she found herself leaning away from her brother. No one spoke as they drove, and the only break to the silence came from Kalix and Elrick discussing directions.

"He's in the city, that's where we have to take them," Elrick said from behind the steering wheel. It was the first clear thing Maggie had been able to make out from their conversation.

"That doesn't make it a good idea. It's crawling with Remos." Kalix glanced back at Wick before returning her eyes to the road.

"We slip in and out of the city all the time without being noticed. This'll be no different."

"If we're going to the city, wouldn't it be faster to go through New Jersey?" Ryker was particularly loud in comparison to their whispering.

They both glanced back at him.

"Actually, it wouldn't. Remo activity has been particularly intense in New Jersey over the last few weeks. It's worth the extra time on the road to avoid it," Kalix said snidely.

She turned the radio on and the conversation came to an abrupt end. It was a couple hours later when the city appeared in the distance, rising above the highway in the way only New York City could. It was unlike anything Maggie had seen before. The buildings towered above one another, in all different shapes and sizes, and yet it still spread like an ever-expanding creature. They drove across a long bridge and then they were on the city streets. Some of the buildings were nice and well kept, but then the next block was run down and destroyed – it was impossible to determine if they were in a Resistance-friendly area.

After several turns, they finally stopped in front of a large brownstone. Only as they got out of the SUV did Maggie notice how deserted the streets were. Aside from the hum of traffic in the distance, an eerie silence hung over the street.

"Who are we meeting here?" she asked.

"Your next guide." Elrick stared at the dark building.

"You mean you were only responsible for that short distance?" Wick laughed. "Blackwood could've done that."

Kalix turned toward him with threatening eyes. "It may have seemed like an uneventful drive, but that's only because you have no idea how dangerous New York is."

"Something's not right. It's too quiet," Ryker said.

"Kid's right. We should go to plan B." Elrick nodded.

Maggie saw him right as the others did. A man, who looked to be homeless, was walking slowly toward them. His face was smudged with dirt and his hair was matted down, but neither distracted from his worn, dirty clothes. Still, as Maggie watched him get closer, she was certain she saw a fire in his eyes, a calculating mind. Her muscles tensed.

"Why hello there," he said.

"What do you want?" Ryker stood ready to strike if necessary.

"Can you tell me what happens when a cat howls at the full moon?" He looked hard at each of their faces.

Maggie and Ryker glanced at each other, neither sure what to say to the obviously disturbed man. Kalix pushed passed the two of them. "Roses will never come to bloom."

The man nodded. "That's right."

"Listen, we're looking for someone—"

"There's no time for that. We just received word of an impending raid. They've blocked off all the streets around this area, and the net is getting tighter." The man looked hurriedly up and down the street. "We have a shelter nearby where you'll be safe."

"We have to go to the shelter where Travis Cole is located. Do you know him?" Kalix asked.

"You're in luck. I just saw him at Schwartz's Hardware."

Elrick immediately grabbed his small pack from the SUV. "Let's go."

Ryker shook his head. "No. We don't even know this guy. How do we know we can trust him?"

The man's eyes widened in surprise and he looked at Kalix, who held out her hands and rolled her eyes. "They're new."

"New?" Ryker's jaw tightened.

"We need to go," Wick said, looking at Maggie. She was surprised he was agreeing with the siblings, but she could see the anxiety in his eyes and knew they were in danger.

They followed Elrick around the corner and down a block. Each street was just as empty as the last and Maggie could feel her heart rate increasing with each passing second. A raid really was coming. They moved down the narrow alley next to Schwartz's Hardware to a solid metal, blue door that stood at the end. It looked like it could easily withstand an explosion. Elrick pounded on the door. A small opening slid inward, where dark eyes lurked just within.

"What happens when a cat howls at the full moon?" The man's voice was husky and deep.

"Roses will never come to bloom."

Several locks clicked out of place and the door swung open. Two men stood just inside, both with automatic rifles. The hall was dark, lit only by small lamps spaced feet apart, which Elrick followed around to a steep staircase leading down. Maggie took a deep breath as she followed. There were no inward facing windows, and from the faint light, she felt like they were descending into a tomb. A small group of men, women, and children sat along the narrow hallway at the bottom of the stairs, and they all looked terrified.

They continued further through the darkness until they came to a small room that was filled with several computers. One man sat alone amongst the machines, typing steadily on the keyboard in front of him. The only light in the room was a lone light bulb hanging in the corner of the ceiling and the glow from the monitors that created scattered shadows along the walls.

"Travis?" Kalix asked

The man turned around and gave a crooked smile. "There are two faces I was sure I'd never see again. You're four days late." He was in his late twenties with dark brown, shaggy hair and scattered freckles on his cheeks. From his pale skin, he looked like he didn't leave the computers often.

"Blame Blackwood next time you see him," she said.

He laughed and shook his head. "One of these days your luck is going to run out at that border. These them?"

"Yeah. When did you get word of the raid?"

"Not ten minutes ago. It's been a scramble to get everyone in, but I'm receiving word that all the shelters are locked down and everyone is accounted for. I'm surprised. It's like they're waiting on something."

Elrick glanced at Kalix. "It's him." They both looked at Wick.

Her hand flew to the knife on her hip. "Elrick's right. Raids never happen like this. They never suit up and hold. They're waiting for something."

"You have to be kidding me." Wick crossed his arms.

"Everywhere you've been, Remos have shown up. The camp, the border, now here in the city. That's just not possible. They're not that good." Elrick and Kalix both stepped closer to him.

"I don't know how they're doing it, but it has nothing to do with me!" His voice vibrated in the tight space.

Travis stood up and moved between them. He looked much more athletic than he had when tucked behind the computer screens. "What do you mean by Remos keep showing up?"

"Everywhere these kids go, Remos follow. Blackwood warned us they'd been on them since they left Michigan.

That's not a coincidence."

Travis shook his head as he opened a nearby desk drawer. "No, it's not a coincidence. We just learned recently they've been putting trackers in people and then putting them back on the street. They've been using them to track down larger Resistance groups."

"What?" Kalix was startled.

"We just found the first tracker on a man a week ago. They hid it under his skin and then let him think he escaped custody. Remos took down a shelter in New Jersey and arrested a lot of people, all except for him. Took too long to figure it out." Travis finally pulled a small, black device from the drawer. He plugged it into his computer and typed a few short numbers before turning back to the group. "I need to scan you."

Chapter Twenty-seven

Maggie stared at the small device in his hand. It looked like nothing more than a phone. "You're telling me that little thing can find one of those trackers?"

"That's correct."

"How do you know it works?" Ryker asked.

"Because I built it. We don't have time for all these questions. If one of you really is tagged, we need to find it and destroy it before they get here." Although he addressed the whole group, he stared at Wick.

Wick stepped forward and held his arms out. "I have nothing to hide."

Travis grabbed Elrick and positioned him squarely in front of Wick. "Take this and hold it directly parallel to the ground."

He did as he was told and Travis went to the computer and began typing. At first, nothing happened, but then a blue light came from the small device, first landing as a point on Wick's chest, and then expanding to cover him from head to toe. For a moment, no one moved or spoke, and only the sound of Travis' fingers on the keys filled the room. But then, as quickly as it had started, the blue light disappeared.

"He's clean. Who's next?"

Ryker stepped forward, and they all watched as the process was repeated. He too was clean, and as Maggie stepped in front of Elrick, she felt everyone's nerves on edge. The light appeared as it had for the others, but as it covered her body, she felt a strange tingle in her right shoulder. It started as nothing more than an itch, but as the light lingered, her shoulder heated up. Soon, it felt like it was on fire. Her hand instinctively flew to the spot and she felt her skin burning.

"What is that?" She managed through gritted teeth.

"Elrick, keep the light where it is. You two, hold her still," Travis instructed.

Kalix and Ryker grabbed Maggie's arms and held her in place. Travis came up behind her right shoulder and pulled her jacket and shirt down around her arm. She felt her breath catch as she saw a bright red glow coming from under her skin.

"I have to cut it out." Travis' eyes were tense as he pulled a knife into her line of sight. She felt the hands on her arms tighten as he moved closer toward her. She tried to stifle the scream as the blade was buried into her shoulder, but as Travis maneuvered it under her skin, the pain became unbearable. Hands suddenly grabbed her face and forced her to look away.

"It's almost over," Wick said as he held her steady, keeping her eyes locked on his.

A small scream escaped her lips as the knife was shoved deeper. She jerked to look, but Wick held her firmly in place. "Stay with me. He's almost there."

"I got it," Travis said as he finally pulled the blade free.

Immediately, everyone released their grip and she let out a small laugh as she looked at the tracker in his hand. "Is that it?" It was no bigger than a penny. Travis put in on the desk and smashed the butt of the knife down hard, breaking it into several pieces.

"They're normally much smaller than this. It has to be an old model." He looked at Maggie for a moment before shaking his head.

"More importantly, was it working?" Kalix asked.

"Yes. That's why it got so hot. I developed my detector to over-heat the trackers so we can identify where they are. It's not always a pleasant experience for the person that's tagged, but for now, it's the only way to pinpoint one. I had no idea they'd been using them for so long though."

Elrick pulled out some bandages from his bag and handed them to Maggie. She started to clean the deep cut, but she struggled to get the bandages where they needed to go. After only a few seconds, Wick pulled the supplies from her hands and took over. She smiled slightly as she let him close the wound.

"The outer lines haven't been tripped, so it's possible they haven't entered the neighborhood yet. They might be too late to find us," Travis said.

"Might?" Maggie asked.

"They could've just deactivated any warning systems," Ryker said.

Travis nodded. "It's possible."

"If they know you've discovered the tracker, they'll be here soon." Ryker looked around the room. Even after what had happened, what they had discovered, he was calm as could be.

"Right." Travis glanced uncomfortably from him to the others. "Well, we have another monitoring room on the other side of the shelter. It has access to the cameras. We might be able to see if anything has been tampered with."

"You three stay here," Kalix said. Before they could argue, the siblings followed Travis from the room.

Wick immediately got on the computer and began typing. "Let's see what they do know."

The monitor flew from screen to screen with everything written in illegible computer code until Ryker's face suddenly appeared. "Wait, what is that?" Maggie asked.

"Looks like Travis has been doing some homework on us. He was reading through your official records from the center."

Ryker laughed. "Like that will tell him anything."

Maggie glanced at him and sat down against one of the walls. "So, what does that mean? The cat howling and all that?"

"It's a way to identify people in the Resistance. If you ask someone that and they know the answer, then they're Resistance members. If they don't, you can't trust them." Wick typed as he spoke.

"How do you know the DRM hasn't figured it out?"

"They change it every couple of weeks."

"How many shelters do you think they have around here?" Maggie watched her brother pace back and forth, and she knew he was agitated waiting.

"Loads. There are probably 50 people here, but I'd be willing to bet in a city this big, there are thousands of illegals in this neighborhood alone." Wick turned toward her. "How's your shoulder?"

She smiled. "It's fine."

"The man with all the answers," Ryker mumbled, but then glancing at Wick, he said, "I got a question for you. What was that box that Blackwood kept inhaling from?"

He sighed. "It's a stimulant."

"I knew he was on something."

"What kind of stimulant?" Maggie asked. Blackwood might've been rough around the edges, but she knew he was reliable. He certainly didn't seem like a drug addict.

"Most people use it to stay awake."

"He probably uses it to get high." Ryker continued to

pace. "It would explain a lot."

She shook her head. "He's not like that. He actually gave me some really good advice." They both looked at her curiously and she took a deep breath. "I told him what we were doing."

"What?" Ryker grabbed her arm and wrenched her to her feet. "How could you be so stupid?"

She ripped her arm from his grasp and shoved him away. "Don't touch me." Her breathing was heavy as she struggled to keep her temper under control. "I knew I could trust him, and instead of judgment, he offered up a real suggestion. No one is going to believe us just because we have a bunch of old pictures. He suggested we break into Fullbrook's house and get a sample of her DNA."

Ryker laughed. "See, he's insane!"

"Blackwood's got a point. What do old pictures really prove?" Wick sat on the edge of his chair facing them. He was ready to intervene if things turned physical again.

"Getting into her house would be impossible."

"Not with the right amount of planning," Maggie said. "Look how far we've already made it."

The walls started to shake and they all froze. The hall grew eerily silent as muffled gunshots rang out. Seconds turned to minutes and the inaudible sounds pulsed louder and louder. Maggie opened her mouth, but before she could form words, a loud explosion echoed through the hall. Screams and smoke filled the air, diming the small amount of light and sending the computer screens flickering.

Thick, white smoke began pouring in through the ceiling vent, making her eyes water and throat close. She started coughing, and regardless of how hard she tried, she couldn't catch her breath. Maggie's heart raced as she realized she was drowning on air.

"It's tear gas!" Ryker yelled. "They're coming!"

Chapter Twenty-eight

Coughing and wheezing, they fell into the hallway. A mob of people ran past, heading back away from the stairs. Flashing lights sporadically illuminated the dark space to their right and danced along in sick succession to the sound of gunfire. Ryker watched for a moment before waving for them to follow him into the crowd. It was difficult to stay together while moving amongst the group of people. Maggie's eyes were still watering, and the pain in her shoulder ached, but she pushed hard through the swarm.

The hall curved around to an opening that had been blown into the wall, which created a path of escape into the basement of the next building. The mob narrowed down, forcing their movement to slow, and people screamed and cried as they tried to push their way through.

"There they are!" Kalix shouted. She was waiting with Elrick and Travis, searching the crowd as they came through the opening.

"We need to keep moving," Ryker said, unmoved by the reunion. He took a sharp left turn and followed a small hall away from the panicked crowd.

"What are you doing?" Elrick shouted. "We need to follow the group."

"Remos are after them. We need to hide on our own if we want to survive." Ryker's voice was calm but forceful. Maggie knew by his tone that he wasn't acting on impulse. He wasn't seeking out a fight or to be in control. He was thinking like a Remo.

"He's right," she said

For a second, they all stared at Ryker. Even in the darkness, she saw Wick's jaw tighten. "Fine."

They weaved through the halls until they reached the base of a staircase. Moving up slowly, they listened for any indication there was someone waiting at the top. Once they safely got to the main floor, they followed the hallway around, using the wall as their guide. There was no light, and being unable to see where they were going was terrifying. They entered a large, open room that had slivers of light leaking in through boarded-up windows. Old desks were strewn throughout the space. Some had overturned lamps sitting atop them, others were themselves overturned, and as they moved further into the room, Maggie wondered what it had looked like as a real office. From the openness, it could've been an old newsroom.

"Get down!" Ryker hissed as he ducked behind one of the desks.

Everyone immediately followed suit. Maggie and Wick were shoulder to shoulder with their backs tight against the side of a desk. Lights suddenly appeared in the room, moving along the wall in an eerie dance. Remos had come in right behind them. They were being hunted.

Elrick waved for everyone to move forward. Ryker nodded and maneuvered further into the room, but there were papers and broken glass everywhere. With each movement, Maggie felt the objects under her hands and feared the scraping and cracking would be heard.

"Are you sure the group would split up?" one of the Remos asked.

"If they are smart."

They kept moving, but they were going too slow. She could see the lights getting closer and knew that if they moved any faster, they would be heard. A large explosion roared right outside the building and blasted out the boarded-up windows. The glass and debris shot through the room as more light flooded the area. Gunfire rang out from the entrance.

"Someone's on the stairs!" a Remo shouted.

"You two, take care of it. Everyone else, keep moving forward."

Smoke filled the room, thickening the air, yet the lights continued toward them. Several small fires were growing throughout the room, making it more difficult to think. Maggie crawled behind another desk as sweat ran down her face. She looked back at Wick. One of the Remos' beams was coming up dangerously close behind him, and she grabbed his shirt and pulled him into the shadows beside her.

"Don't move. They're right there," she whispered. Her voice was so quiet she wondered if she'd even made a sound.

They sat with their backs against the desk and their knees pulled as tight to their chests as possible. Even with the shadows and smoke, the growing fire was bringing increasing illumination to the room. The Remos moved methodically, yet still passed them undetected. Maggie smiled before she realized they were trapped between two groups of Remos.

"There!" one of them shouted.

"Move!" Kalix yelled as she jumped to her feet.

Their companions sprung from their hiding places and ran toward the far side of the room, but Maggie and Wick held still. They both looked at one another, knowing there was no way to get passed the Remos and through the door on the other side. She gave a half smile, trying to keep the fear from her eyes. "I'm sorry."

Weakened by the growing flames, parts of the ceiling began to give way and fell hazardously into the room. She glanced toward the chaos. Travis and Ryker tried desperately to get the door on the far end of the room open, while Kalix, Elrick and the Remos dodged the falling debris and fire trying to reach them. She looked back at Wick, and without warning, he grabbed her face and kissed her. Despite her fear, her stomach fluttered and she was certain her heart momentarily stopped.

He pulled away and their eyes met. "We're not done yet."

She grabbed his hand as they ran after the others. The room was falling in around them and everything seemed more real than it had only a moment before. The door on the other side of the room was closed, but now two Remos were struggling to push it open. Two others fought to get Kalix and Elrick in custody. Through the smoke and mayhem, none of the Remos saw them coming. They were nearly there, and Maggie lowered her shoulder, prepared for the inevitable collision with the two Remos pounding on the door. But only feet away, Wick pulled his hand free from hers and shoved her to the side, knocking her off balance and forcing her to slow in order to stay on her feet.

She watched in horrified awe as he ran full-force into the two men, slamming all three of them to the ground. Before they could react, part of the ceiling fell onto one of the men's legs and he screamed in pain. Wick tried to get to his feet, but the other grabbed his shirt and jerked him to his back. As Maggie ran to help, the door flew open in her path

"Maggie, come on!" Ryker shouted.

She tried to dodge past him, but Ryker grabbed her wrist and yanked her back.

"Let me go!" She struggled to twist free, but his grip was relentless as he dragged her through the doorway.

A loud scream rang out behind them. Maggie looked right as a piece of debris crashed onto Elrick and the Remo nearest to him. The force of the collision sent Kalix and the other Remo to the ground. Travis ran past them and tried to pull the wreckage off Elrick, but he was pinned by a large piece of jagged metal.

"Help Kalix!" Elrick managed to push part of the rubble from his chest, but it was obvious he was badly injured. Even from her distance, Maggie saw dark blood pooling around his body. Without hesitation, Travis left him, pulled Kalix to her feet, and dragged her toward the door.

"Let me go! Elrick!" she shouted.

Kalix's frantic screams propelled Maggie back into action. She smashed her elbow into her brother's face, and he stumbled backward as blood burst from his nose. Without hesitating, she ran to help Wick. A Remo had him pinned down and was struggling to secure handcuffs around his wrists. Using her full force, she kicked him in the chest. As the Remo hit the ground, she grabbed Wick's arm and pulled him to his feet. Right as she did, Ryker came charging toward them. His eyes were dark and unblinking. She braced herself for his retaliation but he ran passed her and collided with the Remo that was climbing to his feet behind them.

"There they are!" Several more Remos were running across the room toward them.

"Wick, get her out of here!" Ryker shouted, seeing the impending attack. He fought to break free from the Remos' grip, but he couldn't get the leverage he needed.

Wick grabbed Maggie's hand and pulled her toward the door. A piece of debris fell from the ceiling in front of them, and they both tripped through the doorway. She jumped back to her feet right as Travis and Kalix burst through the entrance, nearly knocking her down once again. Immediately, Travis slammed the door shut and locked it in place.

"Open the door," Maggie yelled.

He shook his head. "We can't."

She tried to push him aside but he stood firmly in her way. Kalix came up beside her, but Travis only squared his shoulders to her.

"We're opening that door," Kalix said. "I'm not leaving my brother behind."

"If we open this door, none of us are walking out of here." Travis' voice was steady but anxious. "We need to keep moving."

"Keep moving if you want. I'm not leaving him, so stand aside." Kalix's hand moved toward the knife on her belt. Before she could pull it free, Wick's hand sprang like a snake and gripped her wrist tight.

"You saw that group of Remos. There's no way we

can fight them all off." Pounding started on the other side of the door, shaking it on its hinges. "And there's no way we'd be able to stop Elrick's bleeding – he needs a doctor. At least with them, he'll have a chance."

"Elrick isn't the only one out there. I'm not leaving without Ryker." Maggie reached past him and touched the door. It was burning hot.

Wick released Kalix's wrist before standing shoulder to shoulder with Travis, blocking the door. "Maggie, there's nothing—"

A loud scream filled the air, bringing their conversation to an abrupt halt. They listened as several other voices began shouting on the other side of the door and Maggie's stomach twisted as she could make out Ryker's among them. They were shouts of terror and pain. She shoved Wick with all her strength.

"Open the door! Don't you hear what's happening?" Her heart raced as panic took over. "They're dying!"

Travis' face twisted in agony, but he said nothing and remained firmly in her path.

"Listen, they're not going to let anything happen to Ryker. They need him for questioning. The Remos will get him out alive and they'll do their best to do the same for Elrick," Wick said. "As much as I hate to say it, opening that door won't help anyone. If we really want to do what we came here to do, we need to move."

Maggie stared at the door as the screams continued on the other side. They slowly started to fade, though it was impossible to tell why. Had they left the room? Had the flames consumed them? She forced the tears back as she turned to Travis. "How do we get out of here?"

Chapter Twenty-nine

They ran through the building as fast as they could move, not slowing despite the pitch black of the halls. Maggie's heart raced in her chest from the physical exertion, but also from fear. She feared the unknown that was in front of them, what would happen to them if they were found, but mostly, she feared what was happening to Ryker. Was he even still alive?

"This door should lead outside," Travis whispered through heavy breaths as they came to a stop.

Slowly, Kalix pushed the door open and peered up and down the street. Even though the sun was setting, leaving the sky hanging between day and night, the glow felt bright. Maggie looked behind them, wondering again if there was any way to go back and help Ryker.

"He's going to be all right." Wick touched her shoulder.

"I'm fine." She squinted as she stepped into the fresh air. They were standing at the back loading dock of the building. The road led down from the main street and curved around to a small back alley.

"I have a car a few blocks away," Travis said. "If we can get to it, it's clean."

"You know how to get there?" Kalix asked.

He nodded. "We can take the alley out. It's only a short walk from there."

"Ok. Good luck." She started toward the main street. Wick grabbed her arm and she turned on a dime, her eyes ablaze. "Do not touch me."

"You can't go up that way. They'll be waiting," he said.

"I'm going back for my brother." Kalix ripped her arm free. "You worry about what you need to do, and I'll worry about me and mine."

Wick looked to Maggie and Travis. "That's insane. We can't let her do that." He turned back to her. "It's suicide."

She smiled and shook her head. For the first time, Maggie saw the person behind her icy exterior. "Doesn't matter. It's my brother."

Travis nodded once again. "Good luck."

They moved toward the alley, now down to three. Maggie could see smoke rising above the building as they moved further away. Barked orders and terrified screams could be heard in the distance, chorusing along with muffled gunshots. As they followed the drive around, government vehicles came into view behind them, sitting just at the end of the street, but they kept moving. They walked through the narrow alley, then all three stopped as they reached the main road. Maggie took a deep breath, stood up straight, and brushed the soot and debris off her clothes. She glanced at the others and they did the same.

They stepped onto the street together and headed further away from the chaos. As soon as they made it to the next block, Travis led them down the street to the left. No one spoke, block after block. Finally, they turned into an alley with a lone car parked at the end.

"Time to get out of here." Travis pulled a phone from his pocket. He typed fast across the keys, and suddenly, the doors unlocked. "Get in."

Maggie got in the passenger seat as Wick slid into the back, and within seconds, they were backing out of the alley. They maneuvered through the city in silence, and even as they found the expressway, the tragedy of what had happened sat heavy in the air. Once safely away from the city streets, Maggie flipped down the visor mirror. She could feel the dried blood and grime everywhere, but seeing it was still startling. Blood was all over her shoulder and neck. Her skin was grey from the smoke, and chunks of debris clung to her hair. She stared into her own eyes, which were vivid blue in contrast to her battle scars, and tears came. She closed her eyes and forced them back. Taking a deep breath, she ripped a piece of clothing from her shirt and wet it against her tongue. Slowly, she wiped away as much of the damage as she could.

"There was nothing we could've done," Wick said, suddenly breaking the silence.

Maggie's eyes narrowed as she glanced back at him. "Think that if it makes you feel better."

He cocked his head, taken aback. "That's the truth. If we had opened that door, we would've all been arrested."

"And let's not forget, he wasn't the only one that got left behind," Travis added.

Maggie knew they were both right, but the guilt of leaving Ryker was burning like anger in her chest. He had sacrificed himself to save her. The building resentment toward Hayden, the DRM, and her mother, combined with the guilt, had left a swelling rage she couldn't control. "We could've tried to get Ryker out. It was one Remo. Those other ones were still on the far side of the room. We just left him."

"If we had just stayed with the group, we wouldn't have even been there." Wick shook his head.

"So you're blaming this on Ryker? Leaving the group was the smart move. He knew what he was doing!"

"Then he knew what he was doing when he told us to get out! Maggie, you can't have it both ways. Either he knew what he was doing, and this was out of our hands, or we're all equally responsible – including him." Wick's hands flew through the air in exasperation.

She opened her mouth to respond but then shut it.

"Your brother was willing to sacrifice himself to get

you out. I think that speaks more about his character than any of ours." Wick gently touched her shoulder. "Even still, I am sorry for what happened."

"Listen, I don't know what you're trying to accomplish, or what the purpose of all this is. I guess none of us were that high up on the trustworthy scale." Travis shook his head. "Doesn't matter. I was given the task of helping you, and I know whatever this is, it's a top priority for the Resistance. For what it's worth, I'm with you till the end."

Maggie nodded. "Thank you." The anger still sat in her throat like a lump but she tried to swallow it down, knowing they had to keep going. Losing Ryker had triggered something. It was different to losing Jules. The only family she had ever known was just taken from her, and it felt like a hole steadily growing in her heart. But even so, Wick's hand on her shoulder brought her comfort. She wondered where she'd be if she'd lost him as well, and the thought alone made her chest physically tighten. In that moment, she realized her family and friends would never be safe and she would never be whole, not until the DRM was destroyed.

+ + +

They reached the Connecticut border only a few hours later. It had taken longer than it should have because they drove further north than necessary before coming to the border. Travis had explained that the main border checkpoints would be on high alert after her tracker placed them in the city. The back roads were worn but deserted. It was late into the night, making it difficult to see beyond the car's headlights.

Travis drove as deep into the woods as they could go, but eventually, the trees became too tightly packed to continue. "We walk from here."

A shiver ran down Maggie's spine as she got out of the car. They had no flashlights or way of seeing through the darkness, but no one complained. Still, progress was slow. Any time they heard the slightest sound, they were forced to stop. Without being able to see, it was impossible to know whether the sounds were from animals or Remos, and as a result, they had to be cautious.

"Is that the fence?" Just ahead, she saw a chain link fence tower above them. Though she was certain the one in Michigan had been the same size, this somehow seemed larger. It felt as if it extended endlessly into the night sky.

Travis grabbed her arm and stopped her from walking any closer. "Hold up. There'll be motion detectors. If we trip them, an army of Remos will be here in minutes."

No one moved as he pulled his phone from his pocket and began typing.

"What are you doing?" Maggie asked.

"I'm going to deactivate it. We'll only have a few

minutes once I do, so be ready to climb."

She looked to the top of the fence once again. "You want us to climb that thing in just a couple minutes?" The fence was easily two stories high and supported by square cement shafts every twenty feet along the line. "That's not possible."

"We're going to have to make it possible. The only way to get more time is to shut down the monitors near us, but if we do that, they'll know someone is here. By shutting down the entire system, we'll be impossible to pinpoint, but they'll be able to get it back online faster."

"That's exactly what Morrigan told us." She shook her head. "How is it faster to fix the entire system?"

"They can just reboot it. If they do that with only one section out, they lose power to the remaining sections." Wick stared at the fence.

Travis looked up from the phone. "Here we go. When I give the word, run to the fence and climb as fast as you can. Ready?"

She took a deep breath and nodded.

"Now!"

Maggie sprinted forward and jumped on the fence. Pulling and pushing, she made her way higher and higher along the fence. She tried to shove her feet into the tiny openings, but only the very edge of her shoe held securely. After several unstable moments, she pulled herself over the top and to the other side. Travis was up and over with surprising agility, and Wick smiled as he too began his descent. It was considerably harder to climb down since she couldn't see where to put her feet, and each time she moved lower, her stomach tightened.

"Hurry up!" Travis called. Both he and Wick were at the bottom.

She picked up the pace and her feet and hands began to move in methodical harmony. But as she continued down and her grip loosened, her weight shifted on her lower foot and flew off the fence. Her sudden weight on only her fingers ripped her grip loose. She fell.

Maggie slammed hard against the ground, and immediately, a sharp pain shot into her back. She coughed sharply as the wind was knocked from her lungs.

"Are you ok?" Wick knelt beside her, his eyes frantic as they searched for any sign of injury.

"Get her up. We need to move. We're too close to the fence," Travis said.

She tried to speak but couldn't. She coughed painfully as her lungs searched for air, and with each spasm, her back throbbed angrily. Wick and Travis grabbed her arms and hauled her to her feet. Before she could protest, they pulled her deeper into the woods and only stopped when the fence was out of sight.

"Are you all right?" They tried to make her sit, but she pushed their hands away as she finally got a deep breath of air.

"I'm fine. Just knocked the wind out of me." Wick

looked from her face to her shoulder and back. "We need to keep moving."

Maggie walked passed them without another word. Her lungs were still tight, so she took deep, quiet breaths as she went. She could feel Wick's eyes following her, but he fell into step behind her nonetheless.

Travis half smiled as he came up beside her. "At least it wasn't your neck."

Chapter Thirty

It was a few hours before they made it to the nearest town, and light was just coming over the horizon as they entered the streets. The town was small and still asleep, making it easy to slip in unnoticed. Travis led them to a neighborhood where their next car was waiting, though it felt strange to Maggie to walk through such a seemingly normal place, especially given how damaged they looked in comparison.

"Did you hide a car here just for us?" she asked.

"Not me, a friend. I had a feeling we'd be coming through this way. The people that own the house are legal and they let us do this from time to time."

"You're not worried they'll call the DRM?" Wick kept looking around, making their already unusual early morning appearance seem even more awkward.

"Not at all."

They finally reached the right house and Maggie was amazed to find the car sitting completely undisturbed.

She was still worried that Remos would appear out of nowhere, but it had become a strange fear. One that never really left, and as a result, it was becoming easier to ignore. Once again, Travis used this phone to unlock the car, and within moments, they were on their way.

"I have an address of where I'm supposed to take you," Travis said as they drove. "I'm not meant to know what is waiting for us there, but I'd like to."

Maggie glanced at Wick, but neither answered. "How far away are we?"

"Only half an hour."

Her heart fluttered at the thought. "I'll explain when we get there."

Sitting for the first time in hours, exhaustion washed over her but they were only miles from her uncle, from the truth and the proof that they needed – the anxiety was just too great to sit still. Her fingers tapped unconsciously against her leg as they pulled off the expressway.

"The house you're looking for is on the next street over. Just a little further down," Travis said as he pulled the car to a stop. They were in a neighborhood that looked very similar to where they had picked up the car.

Maggie looked from Travis to Wick. "Ok."

"We can't just drive up to the house. The place could be crawling with Remos."

"So how do we get in?"

"We go around the back and hope like hell no one

sees us," Travis said.

Wick sighed but nodded. They got out of the car and each of them was noticeably tense, ready for whatever was waiting. The street was quiet as most of the residents were still fast asleep, which only added to the morning eeriness.

They counted the houses as they went, Travis using his phone to guide them. When they were directly behind their target, they slipped passed the house in front of them and entered a narrow line of trees that separated one yard from the next.

"That's it." Travis pointed at a small white house just through the brush. It had bright green shutters, small bushes lining the back porch, and a sharply pruned tree in front of the large bay window. After what they'd gone through to get there, Maggie couldn't believe they'd finally made it. She thought of all that had happened in the last few days, and it amazed her that just two weeks ago she was still living at the center. How had her life changed so completely in such a short period of time?

"What if they can't help? What if they don't want to?" Her eyes were glued to the house, taking in even the smallest details.

"We're not going to take no for an answer." Wick was determined.

They moved to the back door, and not surprisingly, it was locked. Travis pulled a knife from his pocket and jammed it into the door's seal.

"Shouldn't we knock?" Maggie asked. Her eyes darted around the backyard, looking for any hint of movement.

"They're probably asleep and we can't just stand out here." Travis put his full strength behind the knife, and the door popped open.

They quickly crept inside and closed the door behind them. For a moment, no one moved. The inside of the house was more than any of them had seen in some time – it was a home. The furniture was warm and inviting. Blankets were thrown over the back of a sofa, knitting sat ready next to an armchair, and even a bowl of fruit was on the kitchen table. People lived there, and not just to survive for a night or a week. They really lived there.

A creak sounded in the hallway and a man appeared. He stood shell-shocked as he stared at them. "Who are you? How did you get in here?"

He looked like the picture she'd seen of her father, only older. He had the same square chin and full head of hair, though his was more grey than brown. His eyes were different. They weren't blue like her father's but grey. They reminded her of Ryker.

"Sir, we don't mean to frighten you. We just want to talk," Wick said.

The man stepped further into the kitchen. His eyes darted to a phone sitting on the counter and Travis took a step forward.

"Are you Robert Kerns?" Maggie asked.

The man gently took another step and Travis did the same. "Yes. What do you want?"

"My name is Ma—" She stopped herself, remembering what her father had called her. "My name is Charlotte, and I'm your niece."

His face went white and he shook his head. "That's not possible. She's not, she wouldn't…why are you here?"

"I need your help."

He looked from Maggie to the phone on the counter. He sighed and then walked passed it to the kitchen table, sitting down with a thud. Wick and Maggie followed suit, but Travis went to the doorway that Robert had come through. He glanced down the hall and shook his head, signaling it was all clear. They were alone.

"I don't even know where to start," Robert said. "How did you know I'm your uncle?"

"I had a blood test done to find out what happened to my parents, that's when I found out I had an uncle."

"But how did you find out you were adopted?" He seemed truly confused.

"Adopted? What are you talking about?"

"Henry told me you were put up for adoption. That was part of the deal."

"Deal?" Travis walked closer to the table but remained standing.

"Yes, that's the reason he's lied all these years." Robert looked from Travis to Wick. "I'm sorry, but who are you?"

"These are two friends. They helped me get here."

Maggie explained everything that had happened.

"None of that is what I was told," Robert said when she finally finished.

"What do you mean? What deal were you talking about?"

He took a deep breath. "Henry never wanted to talk about what had happened. He only did once, shortly after he was taken into custody. He told me the DRM had struck a deal that if he agreed to lie about the identity of his child's mother, then they'd let the real mother go free and they'd put the child up for adoption. If he refused, then the child would be sent to one of the centers and the mother would be looking at a long jail sentence."

"Did he know who her mother was?" Wick asked.

Robert laughed. "Of course, he did." He stood and walked to a tall bookshelf in the corner of the room, where he pulled out a thick album. "Look at this."

Maggie took it and slowly flipped through the pages. They were pictures of her parents together. They looked happy, just doing things normal people would – going to the park, traveling, eating out. She stared at them and wondered what her life would've been like if the Reproduction Act had never been passed.

"Oh my God, that's Elizabeth Fullbrook." Travis stared over her shoulder in disbelief. Although she was much younger, there was no mistaking her. "Your mother is Elizabeth Fullbrook?"

"You can see why we didn't tell anyone," Maggie said.

He exhaled and dropped into the remaining seat at the table. "Lord knows what Kalix would've done if she'd known. So, what happened?"

They all looked at Robert and he sighed. "Your parents were naïve. They thought they could get around the laws simply because of who your mother was. At the time, your grandfather was Vice President. He was in charge of the DRM, in fact. But even so, he couldn't manipulate the system in the way they'd hoped, or perhaps he didn't want to. It's no secret he never liked your father."

"Why not?"

"He didn't think Henry came from a good enough family. In comparison to his, of course we didn't. They tried to get married but her father wouldn't allow it. She was still in school at the time and her parents paid her bills. As a result, they had quite the hold over her. Henry and Liz assumed once they were pregnant, once they had the baby, her father would be forced to get them the proper paperwork." Robert glanced at the pictures in front of Maggie and sighed again. "As I said, naïve."

"He did have the ability to manipulate the system, though," Wick said. "How else would he be able to do all this?"

"I'm sure Liz thinks you were adopted as well. I can't imagine why she would…" Robert shook his head.

"Elizabeth does what's best for her. She left my dad in prison to rot, just like she left me at Jessup," Maggie said, bitterness seeping into every word. "You've seen her campaign speeches – she wants to keep the DRM."

"She was always such a sweetheart. I can't imagine this was purposely done on her part."

"I wish that were true." She closed the album, no longer wanting to look at the lost past inside. "Can I have these pictures?"

Robert looked surprised, and his eyes shot nervously from the album to her face. "Why?"

"Maggie, don't," Wick mumbled under his breath.

She ignored him. "I want to show the country that there are people in power using this system for their own purposes. I can prove the system was manipulated so my mother could avoid prison. These pictures prove that she knew my father and was close with him. I'm going to get her DNA, then take everything to the media and get my father out of jail. I'm going to get everyone out."

Robert shook his head and stood. "I need a cup of coffee." He walked into the kitchen and, within seconds, the smell of freshly brewed grounds filled the air.

Wick exhaled in frustration. "This is an election year. If we can get the story out now, it will help sway the voters."

"This is the best chance we've had since the program started," Travis said, more to himself than to the group.

He laughed. "This could change everything."

"We already know how we're going to get this information out to the media. We just need the photos." Maggie watched closely as he sat back down at the table, sipping slowly on his hot drink. Her stomach growled, suddenly making her aware of how long it'd been since she last ate.

Robert looked at each of them. "You're not the first people to try something like this. The chances of it working are astronomical."

"We're the first people that are telling the truth. We have evidence," Wick said. He was being as careful as Maggie not to go into detail about the next step of their plan.

"You have the opportunity to make a difference. Are you just going to ignore that?" Maggie had had enough. She wanted an answer. "Do you support the DRM?"

"No one hates that act more than I do," he said sharply. "You have no idea what I've been through. What my wife and I have been through."

"Then tell me," she said softly.

He rubbed his face. "We were approved, you know, to have a baby. We had all the tests done, passed all the screenings, but then we found out we couldn't have kids. It was physically impossible. At first, we attended the auctions, hoping to finally have a family, but those people have so much money. They bid limitlessly. How could we compete with that?" He took a deep breath.

"I'll do anything to get this act overturned. It took my brother, destroyed my wife, and now here's my niece, who looks like she's been to hell and back."

Maggie swallowed hard. Robert acknowledged her as family, and though there was no reason it should have, it meant something to her. "Then help us. If we get arrested, we won't tell them where we got the photos."

His jaw tightened. "I'm not worried about you having me arrested. I'm worried about what they'll do to you if you're caught."

"Nothing worse than they already have," she said.

Robert ran his hand through his hair. "All right. You can have the entire album."

Maggie stood. "Thank you."

"Where are you going?"

"We were—"

"You all look exhausted. You'll stay here. You can sleep, eat something, and then you can go." His eyes pleaded with them not to leave.

She nodded. "I am hungry."

She wanted to get on the road and was certain Wick and Travis felt the same way. None of them wanted to waste any time, especially not while their friends were in custody, but they had barely eaten or slept in days. It was taking its toll. While they were eating, Robert's wife woke up, and after a long explanation, she was very pleasant. She immediately began running around, cooking, and putting fresh sheets on the spare beds. They tried to stop her, but she was a whirlwind of hospitality.

It was still bright out when Maggie followed her aunt upstairs to see where she could sleep, but after being awake the entire night before, it was time. The rest of the house astounded her. It wasn't overly large, but it was well decorated. Eclectic picture frames covered the walls, highlighting all the places they'd traveled, and books lined shelves almost everywhere she looked. She had an entire room to herself, as did Wick and Travis, and the bed was twice the size of anywhere she'd ever slept.

"I laid some clothes out for you. I'm sure they'll be a bit big, but that way I can wash yours," her aunt said.

Maggie's cheeks grew warm as she glanced at her clothes. They were covered in dirt and blood. She hadn't changed in days. "Ok."

They stood awkwardly, staring at each other until her aunt finally left the room. Maggie threw herself on the bed and smiled as she sunk into it. She changed into the pajamas that were sitting next to her and crawled under the covers.

Never had she been so warm and comfortable in all her life. Light crept in through the blinds that covered the windows, but it didn't bother her. She wasn't sure if it was because she hadn't slept soundly in so long, or because she was so at ease, but the moment she closed her eyes, she was gone.

Chapter Thirty-one

"Well, look what we have here." Hayden's voice echoed cruelly, startling Maggie awake.

She opened her eyes and, immediately, her heart began to race. She was in the holding room where she'd last been at Jessup. Running to the door, she jerked the handle, but it didn't budge. Hayden's laughter filled the small space and she turned wildly, trying to figure out where it was coming from.

"You didn't think it'd be that easy, did you?"

"Where is my brother?" she screamed. "Tell me what you did with my friends!"

The laughter grew louder. "I already told you."

"You did?" Her breathing hardened as panic grew uncontrollably. Why couldn't she remember anything? How had she gotten there? Her hand flew to her chest as she wondered: did her aunt and uncle turn her in?

"Luke never left Jessup grounds, and he suffered two broken bones. Imagine what has happened to the others." His voice taunted her.

She shook her head as she spun in circles, frantically searching for the source of his voice. "No, you wouldn't. It's against the law."

The laughter turned harsher. "Do you want to know how long it took your brother to break? Are you curious about whether he tried to hold out before giving you up?"

Maggie ran to the door and pounded as hard as she could on it. She could feel the skin on her knuckles burst open as she put her full strength against the metal. The laughter grew louder and louder, but the door didn't budge.

"Is that a no? You don't want to know?" Hayden sneered.

"What do you want?" she screamed.

"As I told you before, I've been looking forward to discussing this all with you in person."

Suddenly, the lock on the door clicked out of place. Maggie stepped back as the door slowly swung open. Blinding light burst into the small space, and though she could only see the outline of a man, she knew it was Hayden. Her heart raced as he stepped closer and his hand clamped down on her injured shoulder. She elbowed him in the face and he threw her violently down.

She slammed hard into the ground and pain burst through her shoulder. She tried to regain her feet but then hesitated. She was not in the little room. Maggie frantically looked around, but then let out a small laugh. It was only a nightmare. She was lying on the hardwood floor next to her bed. *You fell out of bed*, she told herself, annoyed. She crawled back into the comfort and warmth of the covers.

The room was dark now that light was no longer trying to break through the blinds. Looking at the red glowing lights of the clock next to her, she could see it was just after midnight. She'd been asleep for longer than anticipated and knew it was time for them to leave. She moved to turn the light on but hesitated, wondering if Wick was still asleep. She didn't want to wake him, not after everything they'd been through. He deserved a break, even if it was only a little bit longer. She closed her eyes, but her heart was still pounding in her chest. Hayden's voice haunted her mind and made it impossible to fully relax.

Her heart leapt to her throat when a creak came from outside her door. Every muscle in her body tensed as she strained to hear, but there was only silence. Suddenly, the door started to slowly open, and Maggie jumped to her feet.

"Wick?" She squinted in the darkness.

"Is everything all right? I thought I heard you scream." He looked around the room, concerned.

She shook her head. "It was just a bad dream. I didn't mean to wake you."

He laughed softly. "I was already awake. Sleeping soundly has never been one of my strong suits."

She sat back on the bed and rubbed her face. "We should probably get moving. We've been here for a long time and still have lots to do."

"You're allowed to take a night off," Wick said as he sat next to her.

"Not while they have Ryker and Jules."

He took her hand and squeezed it. "We'll get them out."

She looked at him. "How can you be so sure? After everything that happened to your family, what makes you think this is going to turn out any better?"

"I'm not the same helpless kid I was then. I couldn't do anything to help my family, but I can keep you safe. And together, I know we can do this. We can beat them."

She pulled her hand away. "It's not your job to protect me. I can do that myself." Her tone was meaner than she'd wanted, but Ryker's resentment was fresh in her mind. She didn't want Wick looking at her the same way he had.

He grabbed her hand back and squeezed it gently. "I know. That doesn't mean I'm not going to try anyway."

She smiled and took a deep breath. "We really should get going. We're not far from Elizabeth's house. We could finish this tonight."

Wick pulled out a tablet from his jacket pocket.

"Where did you get that?"

He grinned. "I stole it from Travis' room when the raid happened. Figured it was going to go to waste anyway. He has all kinds of firewalls set up to make it perfect for hacking."

"He's going to be mad when he finds out you took it."

"He can try to take it back if he really wants." Wick raised his eyebrows mischievously, and Maggie could only smile. "I've been doing research on your mom's—"

"Elizabeth's," she corrected. She didn't want to think of that woman as anything other than the Vice President.

"Right. Sorry. I've been doing research on Elizabeth's house, and it's going to be difficult to get into. Secret Service agents are everywhere, and the security system is top-of-the-line."

"When have you had time for research?"

"I told you, I have trouble sleeping. Anyway, going in at night is really our only option. I can disable some key systems and we should be able to sneak through. Still, it's going to be dangerous. There's a real chance that we'll be arrested or even killed."

Maggie took the tablet from his hands and looked at the blueprint of the house. The structure was huge, with more doors and windows than she ever could've imagined. It wasn't a house – it was a mansion, and she knew he wasn't exaggerating.

"I understand if you don't want to come."

Wick exhaled and ran his hand through his hair. "You know that's not what I'm saying. How many times do I have to tell you that I'm not leaving? It's just, do you know what they'll do to you if you're arrested? You're the one they want. If they took you, I mean, I can't—"

Maggie kissed him. It happened before the idea could even process in her mind. His hand gently brushed her cheek, and for a moment, time felt like it was standing still. Slowly, she pulled away and their foreheads rested comfortably against each other. She looked in his eyes and tried to think of something to say, but she couldn't find the right words. She looked down. "You should go wake up Travis. Tell him what's going on. I'll wake up my aunt and uncle. If we leave now, it'll still be the middle of the night when we get there."

He held her gaze for a moment but then sighed and left the room. Maggie could see he was frustrated. She knew he was just trying to warn her, but talking about what-if situations would do little more than make her anxious. The fact was, regardless of the danger, she was going in that house. Too much was on the line not to, and she wasn't going to abandon her brother and friends by giving up. Maggie went to the dresser next to the bed and took the clean clothes waiting for her. They were baggy but comfortable, and fit well enough.

She took one last look at the room and went across the hall to wake her aunt and uncle. They both seemed bewildered to be woken in the middle of the night, but as she explained they were leaving, both jumped out of bed. They walked downstairs and found Wick and

Travis waiting by the front door.

"That eager to get arrested, are we?" Travis yawned as he saw them coming.

"We've been here too long as it is, and we still have work to do," Maggie said.

"Where are you headed?" Robert asked.

She glanced at Wick. "We have a few more things we need to do to get this story out. I'm sorry we have to leave so suddenly."

Her aunt and uncle looked uncomfortably at one another, but they both nodded.

"You're welcome here any time," her aunt said and pulled her into a tight hug.

"Do you need any money? Or a car perhaps?"

"No, we're all set," Travis said before Maggie could answer. She merely nodded in agreement. "We should head out the back, just to be safe."

It was only as they reached the back door and she looked at her aunt and uncle that she felt sad to go. They had only been there for a few hours, and yet she felt like she was leaving home and safety. Part of her wanted to abandon the task ahead of them and crawl back into the warm bed upstairs. She inhaled silently and turned toward the cold night air. A hand grabbed her arm and pulled her back. Robert held his grip tight as he stared into her eyes.

"Whatever your mother is, you do have a family. Right here. We are your family. And if you ever need anything, and I mean anything at all, we're here for you. Do you understand?" There was urgency in his eyes.

Maggie nodded and hugged him tight. "Thank you," she whispered.

She could feel a large lump forming in her throat and released him. Finally, she entered the darkness. Wick and Travis stood waiting for her, but neither said anything as they made their way back to the car. As soon as they were safely within the vehicle, Wick pulled out the tablet.

"Did you steal that from me?" Travis eyed the device suspiciously.

"It was being left behind during the raid. I saved it." He smiled.

"I'd like it back."

"You have your phone, you don't need this too."

Travis tried to snatch the tablet away, but Wick moved it out of his reach. They struggled in the front of the car, causing the vehicle to rock back and forth. "You don't even know what to do with it!"

"I know more about this stuff than most!"

"Guys, can we just focus on what we need to do? Elizabeth's house isn't far from here. Let's get going," Maggie said, leaning forward between the two front seats.

Travis turned toward her. "You're serious about that? I mean, when your boyfriend here woke me up, he told me that was the plan. I thought it was just an excuse to get back on the road." He rubbed his neck and looked back and forth between the two of them. "You really want to break into the Vice President's private residence? Do you know how much security there'll be?"

"Wick's already figured out how to get around it, but this is your chance to back out. You don't have to come with us."

Travis held her stare for a moment, but then started the car. "Let's hear the plan."

Chapter Thirty-two

"I can't believe we're going to do this," Travis said as the car pulled to a stop. The roads had been deserted as they drove through the night. When they were only a few miles away, they pulled off the expressway and followed back roads to the edge of a thick tree line. Wick had been able to pinpoint this as the best place to enter the property. They were parked just outside the security line, however, they were still close enough that he could hack into the property's wireless system.

"Travis, you can still back out. You can drop us off here and leave before we head in," Maggie offered. The fewer people she could put at risk, the better. She was becoming so accustomed to losing people that she feared it would happen to anyone near her.

He shook his head. "I have orders to help you in any way you need."

"You're not in the army. This is a choice you can make."

He turned toward her. "We might not have uniforms like they do, but the Resistance is as strong an army as they are. And I joined it because I wanted to."

She nodded.

"All right." Wick took a deep breath. "I'll go in and hold all the sensors at the levels they're at now, that way, they won't be able to detect us. Travis, you monitor their computer surveillance to make sure they don't see me in the system. With the motion and sound detectors out, we'll just have to put the cameras on a video loop and we'll be all set." Immediately, they both started typing on their devices.

Maggie looked out the window and tried to make out the house through the trees. It was impossible. She could see the glow of exterior lights beyond the foliage, but nothing was clearly visible. A mile of forest stood between their parked car and the Fullbrook mansion. But the second they entered the woods, they would be walking amongst an array of motion and sound detectors, all designed to know when anything larger than a rabbit was nearing the property.

Despite Wick's plan to outsmart these devices, there was something much more unpredictable awaiting them. The Secret Service. Most of these men started their careers as Remos and only moved to the elite Secret Service after years of decorated service. Wick would be able to monitor their movement through his link to the security cameras, but with so many cameras, it would be impossible to see everything. She swallowed hard.

"We're ready," he said.

"Remember the plan – we need her DNA, and we need to film us taking it. Look for her toothbrush, a hairbrush, anything that might have it," Maggie said.

"You're sure about the video? Our faces will be all over the news after that," Wick said. They had discussed it during the drive and debated back and forth.

"It'll be the final nail in her coffin. It'll be impossible to refute when people see us walking through her house, getting her DNA, and then comparing it to mine." Even if that wasn't true, she knew the notoriety would be unavoidable.

"They'll say we swapped it after we left her house, you do realize that?" Travis said.

Her jaw tightened. Not only had she not thought of that, but she was frustrated that he was only mentioning it now. She wanted the case against Elizabeth to be indestructible. "Can we do the test in the house?"

"The time that would take, it's—"

"Do we have the equipment here? Could we run the test?" she interrupted.

Travis rubbed his face. "I have the equipment to run a blood test, but pulling DNA off a toothbrush is different."

"It shouldn't be." Wick shook his head. "The same equipment that can run blood should be able to run anything with DNA."

"I didn't realize you were an expert on DNA analysis. There's a reason we have specialists that take this stuff from objects," Travis said. "It takes more than a simple pinprick. But none of that matters anyway because we won't have the time to hang around in that house."

"Bring the equipment with you, just in case," Maggie said.

Travis exhaled hard and laughed, but he reached into the glove compartment and pulled out a small black pouch. "You two are going to get me killed."

They all sat in silence for a moment. No one moved as tension hung heavy in the car. Although they all knew the truth, no one would say it aloud: the Secret Service shot first and asked questions second. There was a good chance that none of them would leave the property alive.

"Let's go," she said and got out of the car.

Maggie's heart raced as they entered the forest. She was convinced the Secret Service would attack at any moment. They moved steadily forward, and she was impressed by their stealth. It seemed that over the course of their journey, she'd finally learned how to avoid stepping on every branch in her path.

As they came to the edge of the forest, they all stopped, awestruck. The mansion towered above them. The tiered roof came to point after point and created an odd Victorian look that was still somehow modern. A massive backyard encircled the house, leaving 50 yards of open grass between them and the elevated back deck. Well-placed exterior lighting kept the entirety of the area brightly lit, aside from one dark spot near the back door. Still, they could see no sign of any Secret Service agents.

"If we turn the lights off, they'll know something is up," Maggie whispered.

"We could trip a sensor in the front of the house, try to draw their attention there," Wick suggested.

Travis ran his hand through his hair. "That could cause them to scour the entire area."

"What do you suggest we do then?" he asked.

Maggie thought of Ryker. His instincts were always right – what would he do? "We just walk to the house."

They looked at her. "That's crazy," Travis said.

"You could both easily pass for Secret Service, at least from a distance. They won't give it a second thought that a third person is with you. Besides, you have all the sensors and cameras under control." She looked at Wick. "This will work."

He sighed but turned to Travis. "She's right."

"This is insane. Just act like a Remo and they'll believe it, huh?" He looked up and down the tree line and shook his head. "All right, let's get this over with."

They stood, and as casually as possible, walked toward the house. Maggie's heart raced in her chest and she had to force her body to keep from running. As they entered the bright exterior light, they each held their breath, waiting to be arrested or shot. But nothing happened. No additional lights came on. No alarms went off. When they reached the deck stairs, they moved up cautiously. It was only when their backs were against the house's exterior wall and they were once again covered by shadows that they finally breathed a sigh of relief. Only the glass backdoor stood between them and the interior of the house. Travis cautiously peered around the side and then slowly turned the door handle.

"Stop!" Wick hissed. His fingers flew across the tablet, which suddenly seemed brighter than it had before.

"What?" Travis' eyes were wide as he glued himself to the wall beside Maggie.

"The system just reset itself. It must be on a timed schedule or something."

"What does that mean?" she asked

"Every sensor and camera is functioning normally."

"What do we do?" she whispered. They all stood as still as they could, their bodies pressed hard against the brick wall. The only movement came from Wick and Travis' fingers running along their devices.

"I can freeze the sensors at their base level, set it back to where we had it," Wick answered.

"It's too late for that." Travis stared at his phone. "They know we're here."

Chapter Thirty-three

Sweat ran down Maggie's forehead. "We need to move." She tried to step away from the wall but Travis pushed her back against it and used his arm to pin her in place.

"Don't move and keep quiet." He held his phone to his ear and she could hear it engage. He was calling someone. "Yes, this is Agent Mallory. I'm on the west side of the property. It's all clear. Something must be wrong with the sensor."

"The computer says it's functioning normally. Agent, please confirm you've done a full sweep of the area." The voice was hard to hear above her pounding heart.

"Confirmed. Please advise what is showing on camera." Travis glanced at Maggie and Wick, and they all tensed in anticipation.

"We don't have a visual due to exterior light 4 being out." They all looked up, suddenly realizing why there was a random dark space around the house.

"Maintenance will be arriving within the hour to fix it."

"Understood. I will continue to monitor the west side of the property. Have agents sweep the remaining exterior areas of the house to confirm no suspicious activity."

"Right away."

Travis hung up the phone and exhaled hard. "That bought us a little time, but it's going to be hard to get out once maintenance is here too."

"Who is Agent Mallory?" Maggie was astounded by what she'd just witnessed.

"One of the agents on site. I was able to intercept a call from the control room to him."

"The sensors and cameras are frozen at their base levels, but I have no idea how long until they reset again," Wick said.

Within seconds, Travis pushed the door silently inward and they entered the house. Maggie had almost expected to feel some type of connection to the place where her mother lived, but as she stepped into the large kitchen, her jaw tightened.

The extravagance of the room stood in complete contrast to everything she had known growing up. Dark cherry wood filled the kitchen, outlining stainless steel appliances, and a large chandelier that hung above it all shimmered vibrantly, despite the blackness of night. Even the dark, marble countertops had gold running through them and she couldn't help but wonder if it was real.

She moved to a door leading further into the house but Wick grabbed her arm.

"There's a back staircase over here." He kept glancing to his tablet as he led the way.

"Travis, start filming," Maggie said.

He raised his eyebrows but pulled his phone out. They maneuvered around to the back pantry, through which they saw a small staircase leading up. It dawned on Maggie that it was likely built specifically for servants, and she clenched her fists as they climbed. They appeared at the end of a long hall that was dark and deserted. Wick pointed to a specific door and she knew immediately it was the master bedroom. She glanced back at Travis, saw the red light indicating the camera was filming, and moved forward down the hall.

The thick carpet muffled their footsteps, but the eerie silence of the house put them on edge. They all knew the sensors and cameras would be the least of their worries if Elizabeth woke up and saw them. When they reached the door, Maggie carefully turned the handle and pushed it open. She crept in, but as her eyes rested on the bed, she stopped. It was empty.

"We're in the wrong room," she whispered.

"No, we're not." Wick glanced at his tablet and then around the room.

"She's not here," Travis said. "It explains the lack of Secret Service. They probably only leave one or two guys behind when the house is empty."

Logically, Maggie knew this was good. It would be easier to get their evidence and leave undetected, but she was still slightly disappointed. She had wanted to see Elizabeth in person. "Let's get what we came for."

They walked into the room and closed the door behind them. Directly opposite the entrance stood a massive bed with a lavish wooden headboard and two nightstands on either side. A matching wardrobe sat to their right, which seemed to tower above the room, only highlighting how tall the ceilings were.

Maggie immediately noticed a door sitting ajar to the left of the bed. She pushed it the rest of the way open and found the bathroom suite. A large bathtub sat in the corner of the room with enough space for an armchair and footstool before getting to the separate shower.

"This is ridiculous," Maggie mumbled as she opened one of the two medicine cabinets. A lone toothbrush stood in a cup and she smiled.

"Hold up," Travis said. "I don't think that's hers. I think that's her husband's."

"She's married?" She had never thought about it. She hadn't cared. It had been sixteen years since she'd been with her father, and though it made sense, it still caught her off guard. "Do they have any kids?"

Wick looked at her. "It doesn't matter."

"Yeah, look at this. There's makeup and lotion in this one. This is definitely hers." Travis stepped back and held the camera at eye level. "Maggie, take the toothbrush and put it in one of the bags."

"What's his name? Her husband?"

"It's Thomas. We can talk about this later. We need to get this done and get out of here."

She turned toward the cabinet and grabbed the toothbrush. On the shelf below, she found a hairbrush that she bagged as well. Even as she tucked the items away in Wick's backpack, she felt something was missing.

"All right, let's get out of here," Wick said, moving back toward the bedroom.

She knew she'd heard it first just by their lack of reaction. She jerked Wick back into the bathroom and hurriedly shut the door. He opened his mouth, but she clamped her hand down over his lips.

"I told you I was coming back tonight." Elizabeth Fullbrook's voice rang out as light became visible from underneath the door. "Yes, Thomas, I realize what time it is."

"This means her full security detail is back," Travis whispered. They all looked around the bathroom, but there was no other way out.

Maggie leaned closer to the door to listen.

"After I talk with him, I'll have a better idea of where we stand. No, I'm not worried about that. The latest polls are in our favor. Ok, honey, I have to go. I have a lot to get done still tonight and would like to get some sleep." She laughed, and Maggie's jaw tightened.

"According to the floor plans, there's a door in the bedroom that leads to a study. If we can get there, we might be able to get back to the rear staircase," Wick whispered.

"How are we supposed to do that? Just run by her?" Travis lowered the camera.

"Wait, this is the perfect opportunity." Excitement grew in Maggie's chest as her mind worked. "If we can film us taking her blood and running it against mine, no one will be able to say it's a hoax."

They both stared at her, mouths agape.

"We'll never have another chance to get this close to her. You have the DNA test kit with you, and she's in there by herself." She could barely keep her voice to a whisper.

"That's insane. There are probably Secret Service agents standing right outside her door," Wick said. "All she would have to do is scream and they'd come rushing in."

"But if we—"

"It doesn't matter what we can get on tape if no one ever sees it," he interrupted.

She looked at Travis, who was staring at the door. He glanced at his phone and swallowed hard. "She's right. This is an opportunity that will not present itself again."

Wick rolled his eyes. "You have to be kidding me."

Travis looked at him. "Why does it matter if we get

out of here if we can't succeed in taking down the DRM? This is bigger than any of us."

"If they get her—"

Maggie put her hand on his cheek, and he stopped talking. For a moment, they both just looked at each other and she could see his fear. It wasn't for him, but for what might happen to her. "This is why we're here."

He leaned forward and rested his forehead against hers. He took a deep breath and, somehow, Maggie felt calmer. No matter what happened, they were in it together.

"Here. You keep filming." Travis handed him his phone, then reached back and pulled a gun from a holster under his jacket. Maggie and Wick exchanged a quick glance. Neither of them had known he was carrying a weapon. "We just need to take her by surprise."

She nodded. "We can do this."

Travis slowly opened the door, but although the light was still on, the room was empty. The door leading into the hallway was closed but more light seemed to be coming in from the other side of the wardrobe. They followed it around and found another open door.

"That's the study," Wick whispered.

Travis led them into the room. A leather sofa with matching chairs sat directly in front of them, and dark wood bookcases lined the walls, broken up occasionally by a random piece of art. Just to the right, behind a large, wooden desk, was Elizabeth Fullbrook. She looked up, and although her eyes widened in surprise, she calmly set down her pen and folded her hands.

"This is something I always imagined might happen one day." Her eyes glided from one face to the next until finally settling on Maggie. "I know the Resistance has… unique ways of doing things. Still, why did they send children to kill me?"

Maggie stepped further into the room. "Because you're my mother."

Chapter Thirty-four

Elizabeth stared at her, studying her face. Maggie could see she was doing the math, trying to figure out if it was possible. Finally, she sat up straighter and shook her head. "I'm sorry to be the one to tell you, but that's not true."

Maggie laughed. "Yes, it is. And Henry Kerns is my father."

Elizabeth's lips pursed and her eyes glanced at the camera that was still filming. "I don't know who that is." She looked out the bank of windows behind her and then back to the camera.

"We don't have time for an argument," Travis said. He pulled out the black pouch that held the DNA test kit and tossed it to Wick. "Run the blood."

Elizabeth stood up. "You will do no such thing." Her voice rose sharply.

Travis cocked the gun and pointed it directly at her. "Shut up and sit down."

Slowly, she did as instructed, but her eyes remained locked on the weapon. Wick handed the phone to Travis and opened the pouch. Maggie felt a growing discomfort as she moved closer to Elizabeth, but they both had to be in the frame at the same time. It was the only way to minimize debate over the video's authenticity.

Wick took a deep breath as he plugged the testing device into his tablet. He carefully pricked Maggie's fingertip and extracted a small amount of blood. Travis stepped closer so the tablet's screen could be clearly seen on camera. Wick looked at Elizabeth. He hesitated for a moment before taking her hand and repeating the process. She didn't recoil, but instead, she stared defiantly at him while he worked.

"Why are we going through this exercise if you know what it's going to say?" Elizabeth said as the analysis ran on-screen.

"Because this footage will prove to the world that you're a liar. It will show them that the laws don't apply to those that insist they be implemented." Maggie looked hard at her mother. "After they see this, you'll never get elected."

The tablet beeped and they all looked to the screen. MATCH stood in bright green letters.

"Do you care to comment, Madam Vice President?" Travis smiled.

Elizabeth looked into the camera and nodded. "Actually, yes. Although previous administrations may have used their positions to influence the application of the Reproduction Act, my office is committed to seeing these gaps closed. If elected to office, I will work to ensure equal application of the law to all citizens, regardless of position or economic standing."

Maggie looked at Wick. Every muscle in her body tightened and a sharp pain stabbed in her chest. Rage coursed through her veins like never before.

"You should be apologizing." Her teeth clenched as she struggled to keep her voice level. Maggie turned to the camera. "Elizabeth Fullbrook convinced my father to lie about my mother's identity so she could be free, and she did this by promising him a good family would adopt me. I spent the last sixteen years in a reeducation center. And to make sure the paperwork matched her story, they killed another woman so I could be labeled as her daughter in the system."

Elizabeth looked from the camera to Maggie. "Now you have what you came for."

Maggie was furious. "Turn the camera off."

"Are you kidding—"

"Just do it," she snapped.

Travis grumbled but tapped his phone, and the red light turned off. He slipped the device into his pocket but kept the gun trained on Elizabeth. "We should get out of here."

Wick walked to the door and leaned against it. "I can hear people out there."

"Check the bedroom door." Travis looked from Elizabeth to Wick and back, trying to keep the gun focused. Wick silently left the room but Maggie couldn't take her eyes off Elizabeth. Even at that hour, her hair and makeup were perfectly done. Her eyes were steely blue and focused, and it was easy to see the woman's mind was assessing everything.

"You really don't feel bad about what you did, do you?" Maggie had to ask.

Elizabeth looked at her and sat silent for a moment, obviously deciding what to say. She rubbed her chin. "The camera's off?"

Maggie glanced at Travis, who nodded.

Elizabeth folded her hands on the desk, though her thumb tapped silently against the wood. "The truth is, I wanted to marry Henry and I was excited about you. We had obtained the conception drugs through the black market and I assumed my father would get the paperwork we needed. But when you were born, there were complications and we had to go to the hospital. The DRM was notified, and once officers arrived on scene, there was no avoiding the inevitable."

"Why weren't you arrested then?"

"Henry was offered a deal to stay quiet, which was meant to benefit both me and you. There was no point in all of our lives being ruined. It was a hard decision for us, but I always knew I had a lot to offer the world. I couldn't let my entire future be derailed because of one decision. Henry agreed. So he claimed another woman was your mother, my father used his contacts to modify the records, and I was never charged."

"We can't get out through the bedroom either," Wick said as he walked back into the room.

Maggie barely heard him. "You think you actually loved him?"

Elizabeth's eyes narrowed. "I did love—"

"Or me? You let them send an infant to a re-ed center. What is wrong with you?" Maggie interrupted. She stepped away from the desk, needing to distance herself from the woman. She was afraid that if she remained in arm's length, she would hit her, and she knew the commotion would bring the Secret Service.

"I didn't know you were sent to a reeducation center. My father promised me a good family would adopt you – that was part of the deal. I only found out very recently that wasn't the case." She seemed slightly regretful, but it was difficult to be certain.

"How recently?"

"When I was elected as Vice President. As I'm sure you know, one of my responsibilities is to oversee the DRM.

I looked up Henry's file to find out what had happened to you. I was curious. I wanted to know. That's when I learned about the center and that boy they have listed as your brother, which he certainly is not." She rolled her eyes.

"He's more of a brother to me than you are a mother," Maggie shot.

Elizabeth sat up straighter. "I never wanted anything but good things for you."

"Only if that meant not causing you any problems. If you didn't want me sent to a center, then who did it? Why would they just decide that on their own?"

"My father made that decision. He felt it was too risky for you to be adopted. If a family from our social circle would have been the adoptive parents, there was a great risk of us meeting one day. You do look quite a bit like me, so you can understand why that would be difficult." She spoke with a matter-of-fact tone that only further enraged Maggie.

"We need to get out of here," Wick said. "We have what we need to end this."

She looked from him to her mother and nodded. "He's right. We came here for one reason, and that was to ruin you. And when we do, remember that it was the daughter you threw away that did it."

Maggie turned to her companions. "How do we get out of here?"

"Our best chance is down the back staircase, but with Secret Service right outside the doors, I'm not sure we can even make it there," Wick said. "We could have her dismiss them to give us a chance."

"No, they have code words. If we let her speak to them, she could tip them off without us even knowing."

Travis shook his head.

Maggie stepped closer to them and lowered her voice, not wanting Elizabeth to hear. "We should set the house on fire."

+ + +

"How is that a good idea?" Travis demanded.

Wick opened his mouth to agree, but she interrupted. "Imagine you are a Secret Service agent, and all of a sudden, the fire alarms start going off in the house. You burst into her bedroom and find her unconscious and smoke everywhere. Are you going to look to see if anyone else is in the room? Or are you going to get her and get out of the house?"

They looked at each other.

"There will be total chaos. No one will be paying attention to the motion detectors. They'll all be focused on getting her out alive and getting the fire put out. Tell me how that's a bad plan." Maggie crossed her arms. She knew it was still extremely dangerous but couldn't see any other feasible option.

"She's still very conscious. If we just knock her out, they'll want to know why she's bleeding from the head," Travis said.

"There were candles in the bathroom," Wick said. "We could set it up so it looks like she slipped, hit her head in there and knocked one over."

"The fire wouldn't spread fast enough in there. Bring the candles in here."

He immediately left the room. Maggie looked back at Elizabeth, and though she was still reeling with anger, she felt disappointment as well. How could this be her mother? She shook her head and turned to Travis. "You'll have to knock her out."

He smiled. "I know."

"You should do it now. If she realizes what we're doing, she might scream." As much as she hated her mother, she didn't want to kill her, and she knew if Elizabeth started panicking, Travis might do just that. He shrugged.

"What are you doing?" She stood as he came around the side of the desk.

Elizabeth tried to back away from him, but he moved too quickly. Before she could open her mouth to scream, he smashed the gun into the side of her head. Instantly, she fell backward into the desk chair.

Wick walked back into the room and looked from Elizabeth to Maggie. "I guess there's no going back."

"That ship sailed a long time ago." Travis put his gun away. "Help me move her."

He and Wick grabbed her arms and dragged her to the floor next to the desk, while Maggie arranged her chair and computer to look as if she'd just stood up. She placed a candle next to one of Elizabeth's hands and then used the edge of her sleeve to dab blood from

Elizabeth's head to the corner of the desk.

"At a quick glance, that shouldn't raise any suspicion."

"Do we have everything we need?" Wick asked.

They all looked around the room once again. After determining they were as ready as they could be, Maggie picked up the long lighter from the desk. She lit the candle that was on its side and then the carpet right next to it, careful to keep the flames far enough from Elizabeth to avoid serious injury. At first, the fibers resisted the flame, but once it caught hold, the fire grew quickly. Travis ran to the other room and returned only seconds later with a bottle of perfume.

"What are you doing?"

"The fire has to be big enough that they evacuate." He poured the liquid just next to the flames, making a line away from Elizabeth to the curtains hanging against the floor. It took only seconds for the fire to burst along the trail and up the fabric. Smoke rose through the room as the fire spread from one curtain to the next, down the long row of windows.

Wick grabbed Maggie's arm and pulled her into the bedroom right as the fire alarms screeched into action. The three of them ran to the bathroom and sealed the door behind them. Almost immediately, voices shouted on the other side.

"Madam Vice President?"

"She's in here!"

"We need a medical team! Get her downstairs!"

Smoke seeped in under the door, but they could still hear the Secret Service on the other side. Maggie covered her nose and mouth with her sleeve, but it did little to help her breathe.

"Sir, the fire's too big!"

"Evacuate the house!"

Her eyes began to water as she struggled to keep from coughing. Another minute passed and all they could hear was the sound of the fire crackling.

"We need to move," Wick wheezed.

Travis nodded and opened the door. The entire bedroom was engulfed in flames, burning their faces even from feet away. The house creaked under the pressure of the fire and the sound made it difficult for them to hear anything else.

"Let's go!" Travis shouted.

He jumped over the growing fire in their path to get to the door. Maggie covered her face and followed. She could feel the heat through her pants as she just barely made it over, but was relieved to see nothing caught alight. The hallway was aglow in dancing yellow and orange, mixed with thick black smoke. They made their way to the rear staircase, but before they could descend, shadows on the wall revealed people heading their way.

"Quick!" Wick grabbed them both and pulled them into the nearest room.

It was dark, not yet having been affected by the fire, but Maggie could clearly see it was a child's room. A girl's room. A large dollhouse sat in the corner, shaped like an old Victorian house, and pink sheets covered the bed along with several stuffed animals. She walked further into the space, suddenly consumed by it. This was Elizabeth's daughter's room. The daughter she kept. A lump of hatred formed in her throat and she felt the sudden desire to destroy the room that was taunting her.

"Maggie!"

She jumped, her name jolting her out of her thoughts. Both Wick and Travis were staring at her. "What?"

"It's too loud to tell if anyone is out there," Wick said. "I'm going to go out first and see if it's clear. Regardless of what happens, Travis is going to get you out of here."

"No, we're not splitting up." She looked around the room for another solution. A long bank of windows sat just opposite the door.

"Maggie, you're the one we have to get out of here," Wick continued.

She ignored him. She was sick of hearing that. They had everything they needed on film – she was no longer any more important than anyone else and she refused to lose another person. Looking out the window, she saw a narrow strip of roofing that ran along the wall. It wasn't wider than a few inches, but it was enough.

She turned back to them. "We're not leaving anyone else behind, and that's not negotiable. There's enough of a ledge outside of this window that we can make it to the porch roof. From there, we should be able to jump to the yard."

Travis and Wick ran to the window. It was a long drop to the ground, made even longer by the elevated main floor, but Maggie knew they could drop to the deck from the back of the roof. That would be a significantly shorter distance.

"If there are any Secret Service agents on that side of the house, they'll see us."

She shook her head. "They'll be focused on the fire. They're not looking for anyone."

Travis pulled the phone out of his pocket and handed it to Maggie. "Take this. It has everything we filmed on it."

"Why would—"

"Because whether you like it or not, if only one of us is getting out of here, it's going to be you." He shoved the phone into her hand and then pulled the farthest window open.

The cool fresh air was a welcome relief to the smoke seeping into the room. Travis stepped out first and nodded for them to follow. They crawled onto the thin ledge, gripping the windowsill for support, and began to inch toward the porch. Maggie's hands shook as she struggled to stay balanced without a firm place to grip.

"Damn it," Travis mumbled.

A three-foot gap ran from the end of the windowsill to the edge of the porch roof, and there was nothing to securely hold in between. Travis got as close as he could to the edge, took a deep breath, and jumped. Maggie's breath caught, but he landed steadily. He turned toward her and held his hand out. Right as she reached out, an explosion burst from the side of the house, sending debris tearing through the air. Maggie flew off the ledge. Her heart stopped, and she braced for the inevitable crash to the ground. But her shoulder jerked painfully as Travis caught her wrist.

"I've got you," he grunted, straining to keep his grip.

Maggie clutched the gutter as she struggled to keep from slipping. She glanced back at the ledge, only to see that it was empty.

"Where's Wick?" She twisted and turned as she tried to look down.

Travis growled. "Stop squirming. I'm going to drop you."

"But—"

"Maggie! Listen to me!" The firmness in his voice forced her panic away. "We need to move. Wick is fine and he knows that we're meeting at the car. We need to get there."

She nodded. With Travis' help, she pulled herself up, but by the time she was safely on the roof, they were both breathing heavily. They followed the roof around to the far side. The backyard seemed surprisingly empty, and aside from the glow of the expanding fire, it held no indication of what was going on.

Travis lowered himself down as far as he could and

jumped to the deck. Maggie released her grip, landing hard on the wood, though she managed to stay on her feet. They immediately ran down the stairs, however, as soon as she hit the grass, she turned back toward the other side of the house. Before she could take more than two steps, Travis grabbed her wrist and pulled her across the yard toward the trees.

"He's still out there." Maggie yanked her arm free.

"We need to go!" Travis yelled.

"Then—"

Another loud explosion rocked the night sky, sending fire and smoke high into the air. They both looked back to the house, which was now fully engulfed in flames. Maggie couldn't believe how quickly the fire had gotten out of control – she had never intended that level of destruction. Through the smoke, she could see a dark figure stumble from underneath the deck. The fire behind him made it impossible to see a face, but she knew it was Wick. She ran from the woods, ignoring Travis' protests to stop.

"I'm fine." Wick tried to run, but he could only manage a limped jog.

Just as she reached him, he fell to the ground. He was covered in smoke and blood, though Maggie couldn't see where it was coming from. She put her shoulder under his arm and hauled him to his feet. Travis ran out and grabbed his other side, and together, they helped him to the tree line.

From the safety of darkness, the three companions watched the mansion continue to burn. Wick grabbed Maggie's hand and squeezed it. She smiled. They were together, and in her pocket, she had all the evidence needed to take down Elizabeth Fullbrook, the DRM, and reunite her family. It was no longer a matter of if, it was a matter of when, and Maggie knew the answer was now.

Acknowledgements

Thank you to: Bonnie & Paul Wojcik, Roxanne Mitchell, and Brittney Johnson for plowing through the first draft. Your feedback really got it off the ground.

Kyle Wilson, my favorite brother, and key tactical and military advisor.

My amazing husband, Dan Kennedy, who told me to keep going and never give up.

And lastly, a special thanks to my parents - Gay and Paul Wilson. Your unwavering support is the only reason this book is here. Please know that everything I have accomplished has been because of you.

coming soon

Re-Education

Book 2 in the
Dept. of Reproductive Management Series

Kelly A. Wilson

Chapter One

The fire raged uncontrollably, lighting the dark night sky in an ominous orange glow. Maggie Ward watched in awe at the destruction she had unexpectedly caused to the Vice President's house. Her mother's house. She hadn't intended such devastation, and for that, she felt regret, though it wasn't because of her mother. If anything, that was the only thing that gave her comfort. Her mother had, after all, declared her illegally born and forced her to grow up in a reeducation center; in the process, destroying her adopted brother's family to cover her tracks.

Maggie felt the hand intertwined with hers squeeze, and she looked to the person standing beside her. Wick. They had only met by random chance, and yet he'd helped her do the impossible. He had stayed with her as they snuck across guarded borders and passed the hordes of Remos after them. Despite the danger, he'd never left her side.

"Where are you hurt?" Glancing down at his hand,

she saw the blood covering his body and thought of the explosion that had thrown him from the roof. Immediately, she focused.

He smiled. "I'm fine."

He was leaning on her slightly. It was only as she shifted that she felt his weight against her. His breathing was slow and purposely steady. Even though he tried to appear fine, she could see just standing was painful for him. Fire trucks appeared around the house, their sirens adding to the deafening sound of the blaze. Between their flashing lights and that of the fire, the night sky turned to day, leaving only the trees to provide the cover of shadows.

"Where's the blood coming from?"

He sighed. "When I fell, I landed on a huge bush. It helped break my fall, but I think one of the branches stabbed me."

Maggie looked closer. There was a single puncture wound in his right side, but it was impossible to determine how deep it was. They needed to get him to a doctor.

"Spread out – I want teams checking in every direction!" A deep voice rang out. They all looked toward the voice as Secret Service agents ran around the house, flashlights out and pointed toward the tree line.

"Fullbrook must've woken up and told them about us," Travis said. Maggie looked at their guide and could see the tension in his eyes. He was a member of the Resistance, without whom she was certain they wouldn't have made it out of the house. "We need to get out of here. Now."

They moved back through the woods as fast as they could, but Wick's wound made it difficult. He tried to run but each step came slower than the last. He was losing a lot of blood, despite keeping pressure on the wound, and it was clear he was getting weaker with each passing second. The flashlights behind them grew dangerously close and fear wormed its way into Maggie's mind. Any moment now, they would be spotted.

"You guys should keep going without me. I'm slowing you down." Wick panted as he leaned against a tree.

Ignoring him, she grabbed his arm and yanked him forward. They only made it another ten feet before he collapsed to the ground.

"Get up." Her heart raced in her chest. The lights were getting closer and soon there would be nowhere left to hide.

Travis grabbed Wick and dragged him behind a large tree. "Stay hidden."

"We need to move." Maggie's foot tapped unconsciously against the dirt.

He grabbed her arm and pulled her down to a crouched position. "It's too late. He's moving too slow." He glanced around the tree and then back to her. "I can get us out of here, all three of us, but I need you to trust me."

She held his gaze and, even in the darkness, could see the intensity behind it. She nodded.

"Ok. Both of you stay behind this tree. Stay as low as you can."

"Maggie, you need to keep moving." Wick winced as he spoke.

She took his hand and squeezed it tight. "It's going to be ok."

Travis crawled along the forest floor. As he got further away, he looked only like a dancing shadow. He crouched behind a tree almost twenty feet away and watched as the lights grew closer. They lit the area around them, suddenly highlighting how exposed they were, and Maggie tightened her grip. This was it. Her eyes were locked on Travis, waiting for him to do something, anything, that would mean their survival, but he just sat there, watching.

"There. By that tree." The deep voice whispered, but in the quiet of the trees, Maggie still heard it. They were closer than she had imagined.

Travis sat up and, almost simultaneously, three shots rang out one after the other. The pop-pop-pop was deafening and vibrated off the trees, leaving her in stunned silence. She looked around the trunk and could see three Secret Service agents lying on the ground. Each body was grotesquely illuminated by the flashlights now lying on the ground beside them. Travis ran to the bodies and took a radio from one of their belts.

"This is south patrol. Disregard the three shots just fired. A deer came into our line of sight."

"Please confirm authorization code," the radio screeched back.

"031486."

Silence hung in the air and Travis grabbed a radio from one of the other bodies. Maggie watched but couldn't find words. He'd just killed three people. She'd always known that this type of thing happened when Remos and Resistance members met, but seeing it just feet away was shocking.

"Central, this is west patrol. We have a line of sight on the suspects," Travis said into the second radio.

"Say again."

"Suspects on foot heading toward the western perimeter. Requesting all units." He walked to Maggie as he spoke.

"Confirmed. All units move to the western perimeter."

"That authorization code wasn't real, was it?" Maggie stood.

Travis shook his head. "It used to be, but it's old. We need to move now."

They each grabbed one of Wick's arms and pulled him to his feet. He grunted slightly but didn't protest. Each with a shoulder under him for support, they continued toward the car. Their breathing was labored, but they could still hear the radio chattering above it.

"Please say again, this is west patrol – who has the visual?"

"South patrol, confirm updated authorization code."

Travis glanced at Maggie and she could see her own panic reflected in his face. "They'll be coming in full force now."

They burst out of the woods and Maggie felt like she could suddenly breathe again. It was like her lungs had been constricted by a heavy weight that had finally been lifted. The moon provided more light, and suddenly, everything was easier to see. She smiled, but then looking at Wick, her stomach turned. He was startling. His clothes were dark red and his face was stark white. She prayed the moonlight was making him appear paler than he really was. Was it even possible for someone to be that pale and still be alive? She shook her head, forcing that thought from her mind. They opened the back door of the car and slid him in as gently as possible.

Right as Travis and Maggie got in the car, they heard the crackle of the radio once again. "Agents down. All units converge on the southern perimeter."

Chapter Two

"Oh my God, I can't get the bleeding to stop!" Maggie crouched over Wick in the backseat. Both of her hands were pressed firmly against his wound, yet blood seemed to keep pouring out from beneath them. Panic rose in her throat as his eyelids drooped more and more.

"Put pressure on it." Travis gripped the steering wheel tight, but his eyes remained focused on the road in front of them. The car sped along a back road as they tried to put as much distance between them and the Secret Service as possible. They had yet to see a vehicle behind them, but they knew slowing down would guarantee they were found. Even from an increasing distance, they could see the glow of the fire still burning. The crackling of the radio had slowly quieted as they grew out of range, but none of this calmed the tension in the car.

"I am, but it's not helping!" she shouted.

He jerked the steering wheel to the right as they slammed to a stop. Travis jumped from the car without a word and went to the trunk. In seconds, he was beside her in the back seat.

"Move out of the way," he commanded.

Maggie carefully crawled over Wick to give Travis access to him, but she made sure to keep pressure on the wound. "Do you have a medical kit?"

"Not really." He revealed a large roll of silver duct tape.

"You're kidding me?" Her eyes narrowed.

"It will keep the wound closed and help stop the bleeding. Now, prop him up so I can get this around him."

She looked to Wick and knew they had no choice. She took a deep breath and pulled him to a sitting position. Wick moaned softly. Travis quickly wrapped the duct tape around his chest, pulling it so tight that skin bulged around the edges.

"That's too tight," Maggie said.

"Not if we want the bleeding to stop." He ripped the tape free and looked closer at his work. His jaw tightened. "This just needs to hold until we get him to a doctor. Stay back here and keep pressure on it, just to be safe." She nodded and resumed her position as he got back behind the wheel. Soon, the car was speeding down the road once again.

"How far is it?"

"I have to get you to headquarters, back in New York. There's a doctor there. A good one."

"Are you kidding me? He can't walk that far, let alone climb a fence." Frustration mounted and Maggie was finding it difficult to keep her temper in check. She kept glancing down at Wick, and the very real possibility of death grew in her mind.

"I have very specific orders now that our mission is complete. I have to get you and this video to headquarters. It's not up for negotiation."

"You can take me wherever you want, but only after we get Wick to a doctor. Look at him!" Although he was still conscious, his breathing was labored and grew raspier by the minute.

"You should go without me," Wick said. His voice was so soft, it was difficult to hear. "I'm only slowing you down."

"We didn't just get you out of there to leave you behind now," she snapped. "Travis, what other options do we have?"

He exhaled hard. "We could drive across, but that's going to be near impossible. I'm not sure if you realize, but the entire DRM is going to be after us now. We just broke into the Vice President's house, assaulted her, and lit it on fire." Condescension hung on every word.

"Don't talk to me like I don't understand what we've done!" Her voice vibrated off the interior of the car.

Travis' grip tightened on the steering wheel. "The only thing I can think of is to reprogram our IDs and get to the border as soon as possible. If we're lucky, we can cross before they're able to get our pictures out to every official in the country."

Her anger softened as she thought of her ID. She had been so naïve such a short time ago. "I don't have one."

He glanced from the road to her. "What do you mean?"

"When we first escaped from Jessup, we sold them on the street."

"You have to be kidding me." He laughed darkly. "That's literally one of the dumbest things you could possibly do."

"I'm sorry, they don't exactly give you a do's and don'ts guide to joining the Resistance."

"I thought you weren't a member of the Resistance."

She sighed. "I'm not, which means I don't have to take orders from you. Now, we can either have a productive discussion or you can drop Wick and me at a car, and we'll figure it out ourselves."

"He'd be dead before you could—" Travis cut himself off and exhaled. He punched the steering wheel, putting Maggie even more on edge. The car continued speeding down the back road and as cement gave way to dirt, they jostled around with every bump.

"All right. I can get you a new ID."

"How?" Wick asked.

"It doesn't matter. We'll get you a new ID, get a doctor to look at him and then we'll cross the border. Agreed?"

Maggie glanced back at Wick. His eyes were wide and it was obvious this deal made him uncomfortable. He'd told her before how difficult it was to get a new ID, but she also feared waiting to find him a doctor. She was willing to take the risk if it meant he'd get the help he needed. She looked at Travis. "Agreed."

+ + +

They drove in silence for another hour. Maggie watched as the sun slowly rose over the horizon, but she couldn't see its beauty. She could only see it as a bright light threatening to expose them to anyone that looked their way. She never would have guessed that darkness would suddenly become so comforting. Looking back at Wick, she was relieved that he was still awake. He smiled at her and she forced her lips upward, but she knew how awkward and forced it looked.

Travis pulled off the main road and wound through the woods until, suddenly, an old farmhouse came into view. It was two stories with a porch that wrapped around the side. The white paint was chipping away, and it looked like the property had long been abandoned.

"What is this place?" she asked.

"It's a Resistance safe house. One of only a couple here in Connecticut. Most have been found and destroyed."

The car pulled to a stop and they got out. As soon as their doors were shut, the front door of the house flew open and two men armed with rifles ran out.

"Hands up!"

"Who are you? What are you doing?"

"Relax." Travis was calm, though his hands were up. "I'm Travis Dack. I run out of the Resistance in New York. I've been here before with Delvaux."

The two men exchanged a look, obviously recognizing the names.

"No one said you'd be coming," one of the men said, but he didn't lower his weapon. "We heard you were in the state but they said you were supposed to go directly back to the city."

"I have an injured man in the back. We need a doctor."

They exchanged another look, then lowered their weapons. Immediately, Travis and Maggie helped Wick out of the car. When the men saw the blood, they ran into the house and she could hear them shouting for the doctor.

"In here," one of the men called. He pushed papers off a table, where they were able to lay him down. "Doc, get in here!"

"How are you doing?" Maggie asked, looking from Wick's face to his side.

He smiled. "I'm fine." But his voice was weak and his eyes were glossy.

"Hurry up! Where's the doctor?" she shouted.

"I'm right here. The name's Lou." He walked up to the table and Maggie was forced to step back to give him space. Although Lou looked disheveled, wearing clothes that were easily two sizes too big with long, greasy hair, he moved with a level of confidence that gave her some relief. He cut off Wick's shirt and inspected the wound. He went to work, pulling bandages and other supplies from a bag by his feet.

She looked around the room, finally taking it all in. The walls and floor were as rundown as the exterior of the house, and aside from the computer equipment in the back corner of the room, nothing indicated people lived at the location. Just opposite the table where Wick lay, sat an old sofa with torn fabric and stuffing hanging out. Two winged back chairs of similar age sat perpendicular to it, and it amazed Maggie to see that everything held a thick layer of dust.

"Travis, what are you doing here? You know he's going to be mad that you didn't go straight through."

Maggie turned toward the man. He held his rifle in the crook of his arm, seemingly relaxed. His grey-brown hair was cropped short, and along with his full mustache, gave him a southern look despite his accent being very much from New England. Something about him put her on edge. "Who are you?"

He leaned back and looked from Travis to her. "I could ask you the same thing."

"She's just—" Travis started.

"I'm Maggie Ward," she interrupted.

The man looked to Travis. "She's kidding, right? This is her?"

Travis ran his hand through his hair and just nodded.

"Wow, right here in front of me. We heard what you're

doing and we're rooting for you, girlie."

"Who are you?" Her voice rose in anger.

"Oh, sorry, name's Jeff Conroy. I mean this as a compliment, but you're not exactly what I pictured. Then again, I'm sure you're not normally covered in dirt and blood."

"You'd be surprised," Travis mumbled. He walked to the sofa and fell into it. A cloud of dust rose around him, but he didn't notice. "Listen, we need you to do us a favor while we're here. Once Lou's fixed up our boy over there, we need to get out of here. Obviously can't walk across the border with him, so we're going to drive."

"You can't—"

"It's what we're doing," Maggie interrupted. "I need an ID that we can reprogram. Can you get it for us?"

Jeff took two large strides toward her and grabbed her wrist. Roughly, he pushed her sleeve up and revealed the scar that sat where the ID previously had. "You let someone take it out?"

"She sold it." Travis closed his eyes as he rubbed his forehead.

She yanked her arm free. "Can you get one or not?"

Jeff laughed. "You say it like I can just run down to the corner store and pick one up. Do you want a couple extras while you're at it? Maybe you could just change them out on a daily basis for extra security."

"I don't need all the sarcasm. Can you do it or not?"

Jeff looked at Travis. "She's a little spitfire, isn't she? No wonder he wants to use her." He turned back to her and touched her cheek. "Need to learn to be a bit more polite, though. Didn't your parents teach you any manners?"

She shoved him back, but he merely laughed as he stumbled away from her. A shiver ran down her spine and her heart raced in her chest. "Do not touch me."

"A lot more polite." He laughed harder.

Maggie looked away, trying to keep her temper under control, and saw a pistol sitting on the end of the table by Wick's feet. She tried to calm herself but it was no use. Wick suddenly screamed and her heart leapt to her throat. Lou waved her off before she could ask, and her eyes immediately fell back on the pistol. She'd had enough. She took a quiet, deep breath and snatched the weapon. Her hand was steady as she turned toward Jeff and pointed it directly at him. Instantly, he stopped laughing.

About the Author

Kelly A. Wilson is an advertising executive currently living in southeast Michigan. When not writing, she can be found exploring lost trails with her faithful sidekick Atlas, attempting to bake something with chocolate, or going on an unplanned adventure with her favorite guy.

Made in the USA
Middletown, DE
21 July 2019